ONE SHOT AT THE SPHINX

The Narvan · Book 0

Jean Davis

Jean Davis 2024

ONE SHOT AT THE SPHINX: The Narvan Book 0

www.jeandavisauthor.com

ISBN-13:   978-8-9850814-9-7 (print)
                978-1-962708-04-3 (ebook)

First Edition: March 2024

Published by StreamlineDesign LLC

Also by Jean Davis

Sahmara
The Last God
A Broken Race
Destiny Pills and Space Wizards
Dreams of Stars and Lies
Not Another Bard's Tale
Everyone Dies
Spindelkin
Frayed

The Narvan

One Shot at the Sphinx
Trust
The Minor Years
Chain of Gray
Bound in Blue
Seeker
Tears of the Tyrant

ONE

The Jalvian soldiers at the bar were just getting started for the night, pouring drinks down their throats to the glee of The Sphinx's owner. Jenner, the pronounceable version of his name that he allowed us to use, filled cups with a gleaming smile on his charred-looking face as the large blonde soldiers swiped their credit chips. Soon enough, they would start brawling. Then I'd have to leave my drink and my dinner companion and get to work.

Peter nodded toward a couple of Jalvian officers talking quietly two tables over. "Is it them, Anastassia?"

"I told you, I'm not spying on anyone specific," I whispered. "I'm just supposed to report anything interesting I overhear."

Jalvians appeared to have all been hatched from the same mold, perhaps genetically manipulated to adhere to a standard. Though there were a few outliers, probably half-breeds like I was pretending to be, the majority had bright blue eyes, varying shades of blonde hair, pale-skin, and were tall and thick with muscle. They sat throughout the bar in clusters, their blue uniforms, many dripping with commendations, further set them apart from our usual clientele.

I had a feeling they weren't allowed to drink on their own ships because they really got into it here on the station. Thanks to the flowing alcohol, they chatted boisterously. I pinned my gaze on Peter's face while I struggled to make out anything useful in their confounding language.

"Any favorable progress with your Jalvian lessons?" Peter asked, smirking.

I swore at him in Jalvian. "That's about the extent of it."

He laughed. "I have no idea what you said, but your accent is improving."

"You wouldn't be laughing if you understood it."

He laughed harder.

"It's not funny. I didn't want this damned job, but I'm trying to be useful."

I'd joined the Verian army five years ago when I was at loose ends, hoping to find a new family to replace the two I'd already lost. My father and brother had died in one of the first Jalvian tests of Veria Prime's defenses ten years ago, leaving me an orphan at fourteen. My telepathy qualified me to undergo training on Veria Prime, where rare gifts like mine were revered. It beat being looked on suspiciously by other humans, as I had most of my life. Just when I'd thought I'd found my calling and was settling into the idea of being a Seeker for the Verian people, I'd been cast out after five years of training for lack of a pure enough heart.

Spying didn't require a heart.

"It's not my fault that the only language lessons I got were two weeks with an angry, dying Jalvian prisoner. At least he bought my cover as a human Jalvian half-breed trying to make a name for herself."

"You do make a better Jalvian bastard than any Verian."

He was right, the Verians, being half the size of Jalvians had no hope of being passable spies. Even more than their appearance, their kind and passive ways were no match for the aggressive race who had turned from occasional raiders to outright invaders, plundering Veria Prime for food and other resources to help with the war they were raging in their own star system.

"Really though, how much name-making does conquering a peaceful race on a mostly unarmed world offer?" he asked.

"Not much," I grumbled. "Without a crew to gain me any commendations and unassociated with any Jalvian family name of any ranking, I'm relying on my charming personality to get anywhere."

Peter snorted.

"Hey, Jalvians like me. We have a lot in common."

"Which worlds have you invaded lately?"

"For the record," I nodded to two tables of the Jalvian soldiers I often sat with, "most of them don't want to be here anymore than we want them here. They're just following orders. And I was referring to drinking and punching things, not invading, smartass."

"With charms like yours, it's hard to understand why you're still single," he said, trying to maintain a straight face but utterly failing.

I managed to hold a glare for a few seconds before chuckling. "I don't see your charms fixing your single status either."

"Married to my job isn't single," he said, winking.

"Yes, well, I'm still looking for the right job to settle down with."

Peter nodded and set about finishing the last few bites of his dinner.

"I heard you helped Parishnev broker some sort of treaty?" Peter asked.

"It seems I have more knowledge of the Narvan than anyone else here, not counting them." I gestured to the Jalvians around us. "Figured I could put some of my Seeker negotiation training to use."

"Good to see your years on Veria Prime paying off."

Negotiating with an invading force wasn't how I'd ever planned to use the widely varied social assistance lessons Seeker Res had drilled into my head. If all had gone well, I'd now be serving a city on Veria Prime in gilded robes and bearing a scalp covered in tattoos while I guided my assigned citizens through lives of health and peace.

But it hadn't gone well.

The army had assigned me to the Verian station's citizens. It felt good to use my skills to protect this station where I'd lived off and on for much of my life.

"Because of that treaty, you won't see any of the Verian army here, which means the security team is running ragged on their own."

One of his brows quirked.

"Human Jalvian half-breeds don't count."

He shook his head. "If I hadn't seen a Jalvian before, I'd think you made a passable one, but I hope your cover is something along the lines of having a Jalvian great grandparent. You've got the right skin-tone and general thick build, but you're missing the blue eyes, haughty attitude, several inches, and about a hundred and fifty pounds. And the language, let's not forget that."

I glared at Peter. Thick? I had muscle. He did not.

"It's a good thing most of them have to resort to speaking Trade here on the station since none of the rest of you speak Jalvian either."

"I take it back. You can do a passable impression of their attitude." Peter winked.

"Your turn." I pointed at my empty glass.

After tossing back the rest of his, he made his way to the far end of the bar, away from most of the laughing and fist-thumping soldiers. Jenner, with his black, crackled skin, made Peter look just as Jalvian as me, but Peter's dark hair and eyes set him distinctly apart. Most of the other humans in the station crew had dark skin like Parishnev. The station commander and my captain had agreed that I was the best option.

So, I did my job, hoping to make some sort of difference. It sure didn't feel like I was though. We'd been under Jalvian occupation for months and nothing had changed beyond establishing this treaty. Our station might be able to breathe a little now, but the Verian worlds were still losing food and resources every day, and even though the fighting had ended, more than a few Verians had lost their lives to Jalvian tempers.

I passed along juicy tidbits that I hoped were helpful to someone along the line, but I didn't see much point in it all. It wasn't like the Verian army was going to rise up and fight back. We'd had our chance, and only two days into the full Jalvian force arriving, the entire world had surrendered. Hell, the whole fucking Verian Cluster had surrendered. The Jalvian attack, both in the stars and on the ground, had been brutally efficient. Now all our resources were being shipped off to the Narvan, a star system only a jump gate away.

I'd been there a few times with my father and brother on their covert efforts to observe farming techniques and explore new crops. We'd stuck to the small neutral and fertile world of Frique, staying clear of the conflict raging between the Jalvian and Artorian halves of the Narvan. Now that conflict had followed me here, fucking up everything I'd known and loved.

Peter set a fresh drink in front of me and sat to sip his. I took a drink and scowled at the glass.

"Water? I thought we were drinking."

"I have a surgery to perform in the morning and you, my dear friend, are supposed to be working."

"I can work and drink at the same time. It sells the cover, you know?"

"You already look like you want to fight someone tonight, so maybe just stick with the water." He held up a hand. "I know you can take care of yourself, but I don't want a midnight call into work to patch you up. Like I said, surgery in the morning. I need my sleep."

"I'll keep my bleeding to a minimum."

He laughed. "I don't know how you put up with them."

"The Jalvians? I spent years hating them for killing my family. Seeker Res helped me through that. The entire race didn't kill them. Just like they don't all agree with what they're ordered to do here. Don't get me wrong, if I happen upon whoever was directly involved, all my Seeker training is getting set aside in a heartbeat."

"Understandable."

One table full of Jalvians burst into rowdy laughter. I could hear palms slapping the table over the music from where we sat. One of them caught my gaze and smiled. I raised my glass and smiled back.

We'd connected a few highly enjoyable times outside of my spy duties.

I shrugged. "Don't get me wrong, there's a fair number of assholes I can't wait to get rid of, but there are a few fun ones that keep my nights interesting."

Peter rolled his eyes. "One day, those dangerous tastes of yours are going to bite you in the ass."

"You're probably right, but when was the last time you had some pleasurable excitement?"

"It's been..." Peter's mouth dropped open. "What's he doing here?"

I turned from checking on my marks at the bar, who were just about primed for me to mingle with. One of the Artorian soldiers, who had made an emergency request to board the day before, stood at the entrance. He took a hesitant step inside.

"Part of the treaty. The station is allowed to offer aid to anyone without repercussion. A neutral zone. That zone does not include the Verian worlds, but we got the Jalvians to concede to the station."

"See, your training isn't as useless as you make it out to be," he said.

"Not pure enough for the Verians, but still attempting to do good."

Peter reached out to pat my hand. He smiled softly.

He wouldn't be smiling and neither would Seeker Res if either of them knew that I employed my oh-so-revered gift of telepathy to probe the Jalvians for information once they were inebriated enough not to notice. I didn't need to speak fluently for that. Images worked well enough in a pinch.

While the treaty allowed the Artorians refuge while their ship was repaired, walking into the bar full of Jalvians was pushing the line of tolerance. He would have been far wiser to stay in the suite he and his crew had been assigned.

The Artorian, dark in every way that the Jalvians were fair, appeared an equal match for any of the hulking soldiers who had fallen silent. They eyed him up like one of Jenner's appetizer platters. The one small thing I gave the idiot credit for was that he was out of uniform. No one else in the room shared my assessment. Even the officers at the table beside us stood.

"I should probably..." I nodded toward the impending situation.

"Right. I'll contact security," Peter offered.

As I walked away, I heard him say, "I mean it, Anastassia. I have surgery in the morning."

I waved him off and planted myself at the bar where I could monitor things with Jenner while we waited for station security.

"Ballsy move," Jenner muttered as I sat down.

"Me or the shadow and glower at the end of the bar giving you the serve-me-now stare?"

"Both." He shook his head and went to serve the Artorian. At least he'd make a few credits off the guy before the Jalvians made a mess of him all over the tile floor.

The volume slowly picked back up, but the tension in the room made my nerves sing. I sipped my water, suddenly grateful for Peter's thoughtfulness in light of the need to keep my attention on so many people at once. I didn't doubt Jenner had covertly summoned security as well, but the odds that anyone was near The Sphinx were unlikely. The crew was spread thin since the exit of the army and the influx of Jalvians with aggressive tendencies. If they weren't picking a fight with one of their own, they were intimidating the populace. They were very good at it. I'd been taking notes.

When I spotted three Jalvians surrounding the Artorian, who was doing his best to be unobtrusive while he enjoyed his drink, I checked again for assistance. Security had yet to show.

What the hell, I figured I might as well attempt to employ what I'd gleaned. I slid off my stool.

Parishnev had said that he'd made the rules clear to our Artorian guests. This one looked to be doing his best to not engage with the insults being thrown in his face. Thankfully, not with fists yet, but we weren't far from it given the rising volume and the distinct lack of space between the lead Jalvian soldier's nose and the Artorian's.

Drawing myself up to my full six one and squaring the shoulders I'd been diligently working on building up at the gym since I'd joined the loosely termed Verian military five years ago, I approached the brewing fight.

One of Mr. Stare-down-his-nose's buddies intercepted me. I made out two of the words he growled in my face. *Not* and *you*. I didn't really want it to be me either, but that's where we were. I gave him a hefty shove, and while he was momentarily off balance, darted forward to insert myself between Mr. Nose and the Artorian. Both of them paused their insult exchange to give me a look of surprise. Thankfully, the Artorian took the hint to disengage. Mr. Nose did not. He got in my face and started slinging words I didn't understand. Their language was pleasing to listen to, but learning languages had never been my gift. That had been one of my brother's talents. And now he was dead. And it had been some asshole like this one who had killed him.

I stepped into the back of my mind and let the anger take control of my body. On autopilot, my self-preservation instincts sifted through all the vitriol my Jalvian tutor had flung at me and applied it to the three soldiers. Whatever I said made them pause and then take a step back. At which point, I noticed one of the officers laying a hand on Mr. Nose's shoulder. She laid into him with an enviable authoritative air I hoped to emulate one day. The only word I made out was *treaty*. I knew that one, having heard the Jalvians griping about it enough times in the past few days.

The Jalvians retreated, leaving me standing with my back pressed against the Artorian in a space that was no longer confined. I took a quick step away, wishing I still had my water because my throat had gone dry now that the situation was diffused.

"I think I owe you a drink," he said in smooth Trade.

Grateful I didn't have to feign my way through another language—though Artorian and Jalvian were similar—I slipped onto the seat beside him and nodded.

Jenner was in front of us with two drinks in hand before I even signaled him.

"Thank you, Anastassia. Free drinks for the rest of the night to celebrate the cleaning costs I didn't have to expend."

"You're welcome." I sipped my usual, while sliding the shot glass of whatever he'd been drinking to the Artorian. "You got a name?"

"Chesser Ta'set. Ana... Anastassia, is it?" His accent came through as he fumbled his way through my name. "That's not a Jalvian name, so I think we can be friends."

"We'll see." I wondered what information he held and what skills I'd be willing to employ to get it.

TWO

The Artorian soldier seemed eager to have a conversation, far more than the Jalvians I couldn't form a full sentence with. Talking to him would likely turn the Jalvians who were in the room against me.

Unless I turned up with his head in my hands tomorrow. Then I'd have all their attention.

I glanced his way. He did have a pretty nice head. It matched the rest of him. It would be a shame to harm it without getting what I could out of him first. Not that Parishnev would condone murder, even if it was in the name of my cover.

Two Verians in beige security uniforms walked in. They glanced around and then approached Jenner. He pointed at me, shook his head, and waved them off. As if two of them could have stopped a Jalvian brawl. Unless they were willing to discharge their weapons, and being Verian, I wasn't confident about that. Those two wouldn't have stood a chance. I'd have to talk to Parishnev about the lack of logic with his security people and maybe hiring some larger ones. There had to be some ex-fringe mercs looking for work who wanted a more sedate pace than the edge of the known universe allowed.

Chesser tossed the contents of the little glass down his throat and swallowed with a slight grimace. He held up the glass. "Since we have an open tab."

"No, I have free drinks. You do not. And you still owe me one."

His brows scrunched up as he gave me an incredulous look. "But you're drinking for free."

Jenner set another shot in front of him and quickly poured one for me. He held out the credit scanner to Chesser while grinning in my direction.

"Pay the man."

Chesser shook his head and slid his credit chip through the reader. "I don't know where you picked up language like that, but I hope you never aim it at me."

Never. Like we were going to be best buddies for years to come. Poor soul, he had to realize that though we'd allowed him to land and make repairs, as soon as he left the station's space, he was still deep in enemy territory. He'd be lucky to make it back to the jump gate. And even if he did, the Jalvians would have it guarded. While I was proud of the progress the treaty had brought to Verian space, we'd only given Chesser and his crew a brief reprieve from the inevitable.

I hid my weak smile behind the shot glass as I raised it to take a whiff. The fumes alone burned.

"You're going to want to sip that," he cautioned.

Oh really. I drank with the Jalvians. I knew my limits. One shot with this Artorian was no problem.

I opened my mouth and tossed the contents in. The moment the alcohol hit the back of my throat, I knew I'd made a horrible error. Though my brain knew I'd just put liquid on my tongue. The rest of me was positive it was fire. After a moment of panic, the scorching flames smoothed into a burning sensation that slithered down my throat and ended in warm embers in my stomach. That wasn't so bad. In fact, the hazy warmth flowing through my muscles felt quite good.

Chesser watched me warily.

"I'm fine." I was more than fine. Could one little drink make me instantly drunk? The settling haze throughout my body said yes. Definitely yes.

Maybe if I kept the Artorian talking for a while, I could sober up enough to make it back to my suite with enough faux sobriety that I wouldn't get ratted out to the captain. Failing that, I hoped Chesser had something worthy in that fine head of his that would make up for my lapse in judgment. For as much effort as it took to make words come out coherently, I hedged all my bets on the last option.

"So, what can you share that might help me get these damned Jalvians off my station?"

Maybe not all the Jalvians. I glanced back at the table of friendly soldiers. They were in the middle of a drinking game that involved carrying on a chant. I'd sat through the game a couple of times but couldn't speak the language well enough to participate. Maybe they could drop in to trade. Legitimately. Now and then. That's what the station was for, after all, keeping the foreigners who might not fully understand the Verian ways off the surface.

Chesser leaned in close, his deep brown eyes penetrating mine. A tickle registered in my brain.

Oh hell no. I buckled down on my mental defenses. He wanted to play head games? Fucking telepathic Artorians.

Maybe the Jalvians were right in all their bitching about their Narvan neighbors with their mind-jacking abilities. It was one thing when I was the only telepath traipsing about in unsuspecting heads. But that he would attempt to sift through my thoughts like I was just as mentally weak as anyone else in the room? Fuck you, buddy.

Telepathy was rare among humans and only slightly less so in Verians. Chesser's kind, they all had it. An entire race of people who could, if they wanted, understand each other entirely. Instead, they created rules that prevented exactly that under the guise of privacy. Artor could be the utopia Seekers dreamed of, but it was merely another world embroiled in war over misunderstandings and social differences.

Chesser blinked and then sat back. His fingers held a faint tremble as he toyed with the condensation on his glass, the only hint of his sudden unease.

Hiding wasn't my style. "I wouldn't recommend trying that shit with me again. Rumor is that your kind has rules against slinking about in other people's heads."

He sputtered, glancing around as if Artorian enforcers were going to materialize on the Verian station to drag him away for his violation. "How did you..."

"You're not the only telepath in the room."

While I'd thought that news would shock him or at least give him pause, he surprised me by working his lips from near gaping into a wickedly charming smile that made my stomach flutter. Or maybe that was the alcohol.

"Well now, aren't you just an interesting piece of work?" he mused.

"Am I?"

And what kind of work exactly? Maybe I wasn't the only one hunting for useful information. "Says the Artorian who found his single ship deep in Jalvian territory and appears to have taken enemy fire."

Chesser's gaze darted away to dance over the occupants of the bar. Though the two officers appeared to be keeping a close eye on everyone, several of the Jalvian soldiers were watching us intently.

"Let's move this conversation somewhere less volatile. I'd hate for you to have to come to my rescue twice in one night," he said.

Damn, that meant walking. I wasn't up to maintaining a straight line for more than a few steps. Not to mention, I didn't know the guy, and he'd just tried to jack my head. Having Jenner keep an eye on me would be a wiser plan. "How about a quiet table in the corner? Neutral territory and all that."

"Sure." He turned to look around the room.

Since the Jalvian officers had crashed the pound-the-Artorian party, several of the boisterous soldiers had left. The few in attendance that I'd talked to before—befriended, in as much as one could with a language barrier—were watching me with suspicion. Maybe they were waiting to see if I was going to get away with abusing him because I wasn't quite part of them. The rest of the bright blue eyes in the room looked like they wanted to rip him apart, though they were thankfully maintaining their distance. So far.

Chesser appeared uncertain of how to snake his way through the Jalvian-filled tables to get to the back. There was something to be said for the confident bravado of our invaders. Apparently, Artorians lacked it.

"For the love of..." I picked up my pre-shot drink and grabbed his arm. "Maybe if you were a little more decisive, you would have gained the upper hand in your damned war by now and these assholes wouldn't be causing havoc all over my station."

"I seem to be causing havoc too."

He was, but I didn't mind his as much. I pulled him along with me to one of the clean and seldom used tall two-seaters along the back wall.

The Jalvians liked to be near the bar where they got fast service. Jenner's staff had slimmed since the Jalvian occupation. They'd gotten sick of being mauled by drunk, horny soldiers.

The Sphinx's usual clientele, the station staff and visitors traveling through the Cluster to trade, had also been keeping their distance from the brawny blonde bar brigade. The Verians who lived on the station, many of which also served on the staff, were generally a sober race. A few had embraced the freedom of living off world, picking up habits from other races that passed through, but most stuck to their core values. I may have had some influence in leading a few of them astray out of boredom and for the sheer challenge of it.

"Those are some short tables." Chesser remarked, nodding to the Verian section of the seating area.

"Made for the Verians. Not that they're in here much past the dinner rush, but Jenner's got to cater to his clientele." I shrugged.

"You want another one?" he asked, almost as if it were a dare.

"No." I made a show of sipping the drink I'd brought with me, though in actuality I barely wet my lips. Like I needed any more alcohol in my body right then.

He crossed his arms over his substantial chest and settled back in his chair. "So, are you with the Jalvians or the station staff?"

"Yes."

One corner of his mouth rose a fraction. "I thought we were going to be honest with each other."

"That's your thought, not mine. I agreed to have a private chat."

He ran a hand through his close-cropped hair and chuckled. "All right. Can you explain how you have telepathy?"

"I was born with it, just like you."

"You're clearly not Artorian, so no, not like me."

I wondered if all Artorians had the same ruddy-toned dark skin or if, like the Jalvians, there were slight variations in their genetics. Rumor was that their genetics were dialed in even tighter than our invaders. From the way Jalvian's talked, Chesser's people sprang from birthing chambers looking like clones of their ancestors. It was a good look. I could see why they'd want to perpetuate it.

I cleared my throat, wishing I had something to soak up that shot with before my thoughts got me into trouble. Focus on the job. Get the information.

"Your people don't hold a monopoly on mind speech. Verians have it too," I said.

"You're not going to try to convince me you're Verian, are you? Because I'm not buying that for a second."

I noticed Jenner trying to get my attention from his post behind the bar. I gave him an acknowledging nod. He had my back if needed. Noted. The spindly man might not look like much of a powerhouse if it came to a brawl, but I'd made the mistake of challenging him to a good-natured arm wrestle once. I'd lasted all of four seconds. Though I'd never heard him brag about his strength or seen him make a show of it, if I needed help to take down a Narvan citizen, Jenner was dependable backup.

"I'm human."

He pondered that for a moment. "Part Jalvian?"

Like I was going to blow my cover for this stranger? "Does it matter?"

"All right. Tell me about humans then." He jutted his chin toward two brown-skinned, human, off-duty staff members at a table near the door.

I picked at the bottom edge of the metal band around the edge of the table. It helped me focus on making my words clear and evenly paced, keeping my slurring to a minimum. The shots he'd had were lending a relaxed appeal to his features. Specifically, his lips that kept almost slipping back into that charming smile before he seemed to get control of them again.

"Originated from a single world, spread widely. Mostly transient these days. We go where life is good, interesting. Where there are credits to be made. Where we can learn or gain something."

"Learn or gain for you or your people?"

"Yes?" I chuckled. "Either, really. We mostly drift in small clusters, safety in numbers. So probably more for ourselves, I suppose."

"Out for yourself then. Gauging by your comment about getting the Jalvians off your station, I'd have to go with seeking out dissention for the Jalvians or working for the Verians to do exactly what you said."

"The second one," slipped off my loosened tongue.

His victorious grin lit his deep brown eyes. "Seems I'm not the only one floundering in my mission then."

"And what mission would that be exactly? Because if it has anything to do with gathering information so the Artorian fleet can pop out of the jump gate with a nasty weapon to take out the Jalvian's new supply source, I need to know."

"We wouldn't do that. That's a Jalvian move, not ours."

"Good to know."

He licked his lips and glanced around.

"Thirsty or getting a feel for the room?" I asked.

"Yes," he threw back at me with a smirk.

My stomach did that little flip thing again. This time I knew it was him and not the alcohol. I grinned and signaled Jenner for service.

"A drink is on the way. There's one idiot about to come over here. I will take care of him and then you can expound on what kind of moves Artorians make."

I'd hoped for another of his charming smiles, but he had the nerve to look concerned. "Would you like a little backup?"

"Not from you. You will sit in that chair and not give them any cause to think you're violating the treaty that allowed you to dock here. If you fuck that up, we won't be able to help anyone else after you. Is that clear?"

Chesser nodded.

I stood, keeping my hands on the table. Once I was sure I had both feet under me, I took a deep breath and let go. I really hoped I could resolve this without having to make any sudden moves because I was far from sober. Instead of focusing on the approaching Jalvian, my thoughts were quite wrapped up in the Artorian watching me intently from the table like he'd prefer to be at my side.

Wherever the two Jalvian officers had gone, I couldn't see them. Maybe they'd left. That would explain why this young soldier, with footing equally steady with mine, was approaching with clear intent to make a statement that would totally violate the treaty.

"You're going to want to stop right there." I said in my commanding voice that made Verian's quake. It didn't have the same effect on Jalvians, but they did have a respect for authority that I could work with.

He cocked his head. His long tail of blonde hair slipped over his shoulder, obscuring the few badges on the front of his uniform.

"Am I?" he said in Trade.

I planted myself in his way, adopting a solid stance that was backed up by my years of Seeker training and long hours in the gym. Seekers might be all about peace, but that also meant having strength honed by a daily routine of poses to promote agility and muscle tone. They also had trained me how to get into a person's head to see their intentions, and unlike the Verians and Artorians, I wasn't above doing a bit of mucking about while I was there. If Res felt I wasn't pure enough, I figured I might as well embrace what I was.

"There's a treaty," I pointed out while I tentatively touched his thoughts. My external awareness informed me we'd gained an audience from the remaining patrons. That was just as well. Jenner would know the situation too.

"Fuck the treaty," he said in Jalvian.

Those were three words I knew, but my liquor-scrambled brain couldn't sort out my Jalvian insults fast enough to toss anything back at him.

He reached out with a long arm, clearly intending to shove me out of his way. I dodged his hand and muttered an apology to Peter, who was likely sound asleep in his suite two levels above us.

In keeping with the station staff rules, I wouldn't take the first swing, but if this idiot connected with my body, I'd be within my rights to fight back. There were plenty of witnesses, and not all of them would side with the Jalvian interests.

He came at me again. This time his arm ended in a fist that cracked against my cheek. The second I regained my footing, I went for his jaw with everything I had. He staggered back. My knuckles smarted like hell. Damned sturdy Jalvians.

While I had a second to breathe, I got into his head. *"Back off,"* I said firmly in Trade.

I'd hoped to disorient him. Mind speech usually did. Instead, it set him off far worse than before. His face went red and his blue eyes burned with fury. I was seriously considering taking Chesser up on his offer of assistance when Jenner's long black arms clamped around the Jalvian's chest, pinning his arms to his sides. Like the most effective restraints the station had to offer, Jenner detained the man and dragged him toward the door.

"Anastassia?" said a soft voice behind me.

"I'm fine."

A big, dark-skinned hand rested lightly on my shoulder. I let him guide me back to our table, my nerves scattering now that the beating I'd been about to take had been abruptly terminated. Pressing the glass against my cheek did nothing to relieve the throbbing there. The ice had melted. I drank the contents instead.

Chesser's gaze darted between my red knuckles, my face, and the bar. Jenner had returned to his post. I hoped the Jalvian had been further detained elsewhere or Jenner had been successful in delivering enough pain to deter the man for good.

"You seem to know what you're doing with them," Chesser said absently.

"Far from the first time. Station security is mostly Verian and you can guess how effective that is with this lot. Jenner and I usually hold down the bar."

"He's lucky to have you."

"I am," Jenner said over my shoulder as he took a pair of fresh drinks from the tray he carried and set them in front of us. He slid a second glass filled with ice toward my hand. I noted that Chesser's liquor had a blue tint to it. My drink was clear. Fucking water again. My swimming head informed me that water was what I needed. The rest of me wanted another drink or two so I could be numb to the pounding in my head and my hand.

Jenner set a bowl of my favorite warm, crunchy bread knots between us. A small bowl of orange-colored cream set in the middle of the knots. "I even added extra spice to the cheese. Just how you like it."

"Thank you." I smiled up at him, despite how much it hurt my face.

He patted my back gently. "Take the rest of the night off, but stay back here until I close. Both of you. I wouldn't put it past that last one to wait outside. Security and I will escort you home."

"Thank you." While I could take care of myself, I wouldn't put it past the disgruntled Jalvian to gather some friends and try to get through me to Chesser.

I dunked one of the delectable knots into the cheese and popped it into my mouth, chewing on the opposite side from where I'd been hit. My taste buds squealed with joy.

That little hiatus over, I focused on the man I'd be sharing the next two hours with. "You were going to tell me why you're on my station?"

THREE

"Why I'm on the station? No, I was going to tell you about my homeworld," Chesser said, shaking his head and snickering. "I thought your boss said you were taking the rest of the night off."

"Jenner isn't my boss." I couldn't resist eating another cheese-covered bread knot. "We're just friends."

"A friend you take punches for?"

"We exchange favors."

He nodded. "I see. You work security and he gives you free drinks and food."

"And he lets me work and steps in when things get to out of control."

"This work..." He cocked his head and gave me a pondering once over. "Care to elaborate?"

"Not at the moment. You were telling me why you're on the station."

"Persistent, aren't you?"

I popped another bread knot into my mouth. "And hungry. Try one so I don't eat them all." I slathered one in cheese and held it out for him.

His gaze held mine as he ate it right from my fingers. My face flushed. He grinned as he finished chewing.

"I see why you like them," he said.

He ate another one on his own. I found that slightly disappointing. Like I expected he'd keep eating out of my hand. Don't be an idiot, I chastised myself.

Before I knew it, we were having a stare-down over the last knot. Chesser picked it up and tore it in half. After scraping up the remaining cheese, he held out one half to me.

I leaned forward, daring myself to eat out of his fingers, but lost my nerve. I plucked it out of his hand instead. He seemed disappointed too.

Flirting was part of my job, getting soldiers to let their guards down and have a few drinks so I could drop into a light probe and skim information. I was used to using my talents on Jalvians. They didn't require much encouragement, more or less assuming I was interested since I was sitting with them. When the mood struck, I wasn't opposed to a consensual visit to their suite. We all needed to burn off a little steam now and then, and the station didn't have many forms of adult entertainment.

This Artorian though, he was different. Maybe because we were having a more playful conversation than I was able to have with the Jalvians. I couldn't help but wonder how he might be different in other ways.

"I'll make you a deal. You tell me who you're working for, and I'll tell you why I'm here far inside enemy territory on a shot up ship."

He'd be leaving in a couple of days and wouldn't be getting far. My Jalvian half-breed cover would be safe enough as long as I figured out a way to spin having this conversation rather than spitting on him.

"Deal."

"Two Jalvian generals are supposed to meet on this station to discuss the next move against Artor. They're concerned about leaks, and rightly so. We've been able to intercept many of their plans and be prepared for their attacks. It's how we've lasted this long."

"And you're here to learn those plans and take that intel home?"

He nodded.

"You'll never live long enough to get through the gate and you can't transmit anything from here without getting caught."

Chesser's shoulders drooped as he sighed. "We hadn't realized they had so many ships out this way and having to limp here on our damaged ship, I'm days behind. I'm usually able to imbed myself better than this." He gestured to the Jalvian occupants around us.

"Usually?" He put himself in reckless situations regularly?

"Doing everything I can to protect my people is my job, Anastassia."

I glanced around the Sphinx, filled with men and women from an invading star system. "Yes, all right, I get that."

"We didn't use the gate to get here, and we don't plan on using it to get home."

The food and serious conversation cleared my thoughts a little. I could also feel my face and knuckles more. Dammit. I held what was left of the ice Jenner had left up to my cheek.

"Smart, but whatever you learn will probably take too long to get home if you don't."

He grimaced. "It's all I can do. I've got a little brother back home and I'm all the family he's got. I need to make it back, intel be damned."

"And how do you plan on getting close enough to these generals to overhear anything?"

"You're not the only telepath in the room, remember?"

I studied him; an intriguing Artorian puzzle. "Can you touch their minds lightly enough that they won't notice? And from a distance, where you are unseen? And will that light touch get you in deep enough to get what you need?"

"I'll have to, won't I? Anastassia, we need this," he said plaintively. "This war has been going on too damned long. We've lost too much and we can't hold out forever. They're beating us down, slowly but surely."

"And if you get these plans, will you gain the upper hand? Enough of an upper hand that they might have to pull their excess forces out of the Verian Cluster?"

"I can't promise that, but I'd like to if it would mean you might help me."

The pleading on his face, deep in his eyes, reminded me of my father adamantly telling me to stay safely on the station while he and my brother went down to Prime to relay their findings to whoever had been financing his last agricultural study. He'd known the Jalvians were getting more violent with their occasional raids. Yet, he'd gone anyway. I'd begged him not to. I wondered if Chesser's brother had begged him not to leave either. And now here he was, on a desperate mission that was destined not to end well for him or his homeworld unless he got help.

I tested my tender knuckles and found the pain tolerable. That damned Jalvian had a hard face.

"I work for the Verian military. We want the Jalvians gone. Trading with them on our terms was one thing. The occasional raid was bearable, but this occupation?" I shook my head. "It goes against everything the Verian people believe in."

Chesser nodded. "If you help me, I will do everything I can to get them to pull out of the Cluster."

What could one soldier do? He had a crew of three others, but they were smart enough to stay out of sight. The brazen idiot was probably hoping the Generals would be here, that he could find them here and play my game of skimming drunk minds. But that wasn't reality. He was one operative deep behind enemy lines, and now he was known to the Jalvians on the station. He'd played his hand too early. Even if he did get the information and made it home, would he use it wisely enough to benefit the Verians? I couldn't take that chance.

"If I help you, I'm going with you to make sure what you do benefits my people here."

He sipped his half-empty drink and stared at my red knuckles. "If you come with me, I can't guarantee we'll make it to Artor. Even if we do, I can't promise to return you to this station. I have to go where my orders take me."

"I'll make my own way back."

"Trade ships are scarce in the Narvan. No one wants to chance getting involved in our war or having their goods seized by either side."

Taking a break from the station wouldn't be so bad. I'd return eventually, and though it would be a long wait for a connection, I could vid call Peter or any of my other friends in the meantime. If I could truly do something that would pull the Jalvians from the Cluster, neither my captain nor Parishnev would prevent me from doing it.

"I said, I'm in."

Chesser grinned. "Thank you. You won't regret it."

FOUR

The Sphinx's lights blasted into the bright setting, cueing the last of the bar patrons that closing time had arrived. They quickly paid their tabs and left. The music that had been the backbone of the general din seemed loud now that the bar was empty. It cut off to a sudden silence, and then Jenner shooed off the last of the staff. The security bars made a dreadful screech as Jenner pulled them along the track and locked them into place across the door.

"Give me a few minutes to close out and then I'll make sure you both get home safe," he said in our direction.

Chesser followed me over to the bar as I brought up our last glasses. I'd stuck to water the rest of the night and was thankfully feeling mostly back to myself. He, however, had not, but he seemed to be holding up fairly well given that he'd not had any more of those instant-drunk shots he'd started off with. While I put our glasses in the washer, he went to help Jenner put the chairs up so the cleaning bot could do the floors overnight.

"If you two need a job, I have some openings," Jenner said with a wink.

"All set, thanks," Chesser said, his words verging on slurring.

"You know I already have one, but thanks for the fallback plan," I added.

Once the obvious tasks that we could speed along were complete, we hung out by the door. Jenner turned most of the lights out and went into the back office.

"We could continue our planning in private, if you're up for it," Chesser said, his shoulder rubbing against mine where we leaned against the wall.

"I'll consider it." In truth, I'd been going to suggest the same thing.

If we were going to pull this intel heist off, we needed a solid plan.

Chesser glanced at the closed backroom door. Two seconds later, the lips I'd been watching all night were on mine. He kept his hands to himself at first, but then I was suddenly in his arms and pressed against his body. As I did a little hand exploring of my own, I had to admit, he had a very nice body to be pressed against.

A loud thump accompanied the opening of the office door. Jenner loudly announced, "All wrapped up. Let's get going."

Chesser broke away like someone had just poured a bucket of cold water down his back.

It belatedly occurred to me that the security vids were in the back office. Jenner knew exactly what he was walking in on, hence the warning. I laughed to myself, but let Chesser have his dignity.

"Was that decisive enough for you?" he whispered in my ear while Jenner opened the bars to let us out.

Chesser's attack and retreat were both acceptable, and after that warm up, I was looking forward to seeing what else he might decisively do—whether or not that involved actual planning. Now that he was drunk and I was sober, I felt more comfortable with my level of control over the situation.

"Please tell me you're not sharing a room," I whispered back. While I was definitely interested, in keeping with my own security policy, I never brought men back to my suite.

"The suite, yes, a bedroom, no." He grinned.

We waited outside while Jenner locked up. I didn't see any sign of the Jalvian who had punched me, but I wasn't opposed to being safe. We had procedures to follow, and with the occupation, I had no issue with following them when they were in my favor.

One of the security team met us a minute later. "Ready?" the little Verian asked.

"Got the late shift again, Kinny?" asked Jenner. "We'll be escorting these two home first."

She nodded. "I heard you had some Jalvian trouble earlier."

The two of them launched into friendly banter as we headed to the lift. The social district was eerily quiet after hours. With the lights dimmed and nothing but quiet conversation behind us, I stuck close to Chesser. I didn't venture out alone in the wee hours. My job required me to be out and about when people were around to see and overhear. This dark silence was not my element. Chesser seemed wary too, as if he expected Jalvians to leap out of the shadows.

When we made it to the lift without incident, I relaxed a little. The newsfeed vid on the wall in front of us sped through the last of the headlines from the surface and then switched over to station news. General Zhan, our Jalvian overseer, stared at me through the vid as his recording reminded everyone of the current station rules. I shivered, thinking of the long nerve-wracking hours sitting across from his menacing face during the treaty negotiations. If I had my choice of Jalvian assholes to deport from the station, he was at the top of the list.

The doors opened to the first residential level, and I felt even better. The corridor lights were always on here and though foot traffic was sparse, there were other people going about their jobs. Some of those people were Jalvian and every one of them gave Chesser a calculating look as we passed.

He moved closer to me and slowed until Jenner and Kinny were right behind us. "Don't need more trouble," he muttered.

"You could make our jobs easier by staying in your suite until your repairs are completed and then leave," said Kinny.

Staying cooped up wasn't something I was good at either, and he had a mission. One I had an interest in.

I turned to Kinny as we walked. "I'll watch him. He won't be any more trouble for you."

"That would be appreciated, Anastassia. We have more than enough work already without this lot adding to the chaos." Kinny consulted her datapad and stopped in front of a door. "Here we are. Safely home."

I addressed Kinny, "The Jalvians are aware they are on the station. A few of them even know exactly where now that they've seen us here tonight." I nodded toward the two Jalvians who had just passed us. "I'll stay here with them in case anyone gets any ideas. The treaty didn't slow the stupid ones down, and their superiors can't watch all of them all the time."

Kinny flushed with approval. "Admirable devotion to your job. I'll make a note of it on your record."

I didn't have to look at Jenner to know he was barely containing his amusement at Kinny's obliviousness.

"Thank you, Kinny. Have a good night, both of you." I nudged Chesser toward the entry panel next to the door.

Jenner and Kinny walked back to the lift. Most of the station staff lived two levels up, leaving this one to guests. The level above us was almost exclusively Jalvians thanks to the occupation. While I had intended to stay the rest of the night for personal reasons, being the sole barrier between four contained Artorians and a station full of Jalvians put me on edge. Getting him out of sight was my first priority.

"Inside." I again gestured for Chesser to activate the door.

He complied. The door opened to a dark suite.

Chesser activated the dim nighttime lighting so we didn't bump into anything. It was a typical large family suite, four small bedrooms off a decent-sized common room with a small kitchen and single bathroom. My suite was identical, having belonged to my family when it was more than just me. I'd never downgraded, even after mostly emptying the rooms of personal items that had once been my father's and brother's. It was the only place that felt like home.

Chesser's suite would have easily contained the four of them for a couple of days without being too cramped, but station policy was that we didn't confine anyone to their rooms against their will. Security had cells to contain unruly occupants. Unhappily confined ones caused too much damage to the living spaces.

Three of the four doors were closed. Chesser nodded toward the open one and once we were inside, he closed it. The standard furniture was in the default layout. It appeared Chesser and his crew were more respectful of the supplied furnishings than many of our visitors.

I would have preferred that he left the door open in case I needed to make a quick exit. That had happened twice in my adult life on the station. But I also appreciated privacy, given the other occupants of the suite. If it came down to it, I was armed, and Jenner and Kinny knew where I was. No doubt Kinny would make a note of my Artorian watch offer in her hourly report. The Verians kept meticulous logs. Most of them, being devout in their ways, were rarely distracted by anything fun.

If Jalvian's came bursting through the door, I could leave Chesser with my datapad to call for help while I attempted to diffuse the situation. My already aching and tired body hoped there wasn't a situation.

"You can go, if you've changed your mind," Chesser said quietly.

I shook off my hesitant thoughts. "Are we planning or..."

"Yes?" He chuckled.

"That's my answer."

"It is," he admitted with a wink. "Let's plan quickly so we can move on to the or."

I sat on the edge of the standard bed, covered in rumpled generic bed coverings. Chesser settled beside me, his hands in his lap, and a few inches between us.

"How are you getting close enough to the generals to probe them?" I asked.

"I don't think I can now. They know my face. My crew isn't up to the task." He sighed. "I was hoping the generals would be in the bar. I'm running out of time."

"Your crew, are they injured?"

He shook his head. "Using our abilities like I need to directly violates our tenets. I'm not willing to ask them to do that."

"Even for what is at stake?"

"It's my mission, not theirs. Their job is to get me here and back."

"So you're using me to do your nonconsensual probe instead?"

He looked abashed. "Not using exactly. You did sort of volunteer."

"I did," I admitted, even though part of me wondered if he'd somehow manipulated me into volunteering. Then again, did it matter if he had, if I could help end the Jalvian occupation?

"Do you know their names?" I asked.

"Sharta and Nalaton."

"I'll watch the incoming ships tomorrow and scan for their names."

His brows rose. "You can do that?"

"My job gets me access to a lot of things with few questions."

"I have a feeling your talents aren't fully realized here. You could be an enormous asset to us."

"*Us* who exactly?"

"My team. We can talk about that later if you're interested. Maybe as a consultant? Outside contractor? Your call, on your terms, of course."

Venturing outside the Cluster, seeing other worlds, had always been a dream of mine. Perhaps it was fueled by my childhood traveling with my father. But the station was my home. My people were here, humans, but also Verians, Arminians, and the assorted transient regulars who worked the trade routes.

I looked at the same grey-green walls that were in my suite. It wasn't like I'd be leaving for good. I could wait to see if I liked his homeworld before giving consideration to what my terms might be. Besides, a short contract for experience might be an angle I could work on with my captain.

"Let's get through tomorrow first," I said.

"Right. Can your access get you assigned to security duty in the room with them or right outside it? How close do you need to be? I don't know how your abilities work. That would probably have been a question to ask first. If you need to touch them, that might be a problem."

"You think?" I laughed. Tentatively opening my mind to his, I reached out, lightly touching his thoughts. Not a probe, but an invitation.

My efforts were met with avid approval, followed immediately by a heated vibrating sensation in my mind. It wasn't uncomfortable, but unfamiliar.

"What is that?"

His gaze had gone all liquid and locked on mine. Uncertainty made me consider going for the door, but I put a good deal of stock in following my gut, and it was telling me to see how this played out. The door was right there if I needed it.

He must have sensed my resolve because seconds later, his lips were on mine. He returned to the fervor I'd been enjoying before Jenner's interruption. Except this time, the heated buzzing in my head accompanied the action.

While I enjoyed his attention, I examined the mental sensation, following its source back to Chesser's mind and finding an open invitation to sink in further. As our tongues explored each other's mouths, so did our minds intermingle until I felt the sensation of a caress there as well. The caress became a kiss that was deeper and more electric than the one happening physically.

I was no stranger to what our bodies were doing, but I'd never been with another telepath before. I had no idea this was a thing. Wanting more, I rubbed against him where we sat, but also in his mind. In his head, I made sure there were no clothes between us.

Chesser moaned. Electric sparks lit in my mind, begging me to continue. I ran my hands over his chest and down his stomach, replicating the same sensations in our minds, allowing for more intensity than hands alone offered.

Fingers, lips, hands, the heated friction of skin on skin enveloped my mind until I could barely catch my breath. What was happening physically and what was in my head was no longer discernable. I let all the sensations run through me. Lost in the moaning that might have been mine or his. Minutes or hours passed while we exquisitely tantalized each other until I couldn't take another second. An explosion of blissful white light and weightlessness accompanied the familiar climactic ending to a gratifying encounter. Just as I was coming down, the climax hit me again, but filtered, not as overwhelming. I realized it was his.

I didn't understand all the politics that pitted the Jalvians against Artorians, but as I sat there tingling from head to foot inside and out, I was pretty sure it had to be jealousy. No Jalvian I'd been with had ever done that. And hell, we were still sitting up and clothed, no less.

"You could sleep on the couch if you actually want to do guard duty, but I'd rather you stayed right here." Chesser fell back on the bed, pulling me down with him. He wrapped his arms around me.

Most of the furniture in my suite was custom, having been upgraded or bought off-station in my father's travels over the years. My couch and bed were comfortable. These were serviceable and durable.

"Having slept on a standard issue couch, I'm inclined to take you up on the offer to sleep here."

"Good."

He curled against my back, forming a warm and solid wall between me and the door that put my mind at as much ease as my languid body. I spoke the command to turn off the dim lights and relaxed against him.

If sex with an Artorian was that fantastic while still clothed, I couldn't wait to hit him up for the full experience in the morning.

FIVE

When I cracked my eyes open, the time display on the wall indicated that morning had not yet officially arrived. We had time for round two before I had to slink back to my suite to change so we could go steal the attack plans.

During the night, we'd both rolled over and were now facing one another. His soft breathing assured me he was still asleep. I wanted Chesser back in my head, doing what he'd done last night and that required him to be awake.

I ran my hand lightly down his shirt toward his stomach. His breathing changed and his eyes fluttered open. Chesser smiled sleepily. Lifting his head, he kissed me and snuggled closer. I worked my way down to the front of his pants. He froze.

Rather than feeling any form of stiffness or hearing any encouraging noises, panic flooded his face. I quickly pulled my hand away.

Chesser rolled over and sat up. "I'm sorry, I..." He ran his hands over his face. "I haven't been with a non-Artorian woman before. After last night, I didn't consider..."

Were they built differently? It had felt like all the necessary bits were there. From what I understood, Jalvians and Artorians were closely related. I was pretty sure that I would have overheard Jalvians making disparaging remarks regarding the Artorian lack of sexual prowess if they were incompatible. Was there something wrong with him? "Spit it out already."

"We can't perform anything physical until after we're joined."

"Joined?"

He sucked on his bottom lip for a moment, brows scrunching together. "Officially in a lifelong relationship."

"That's some devout religious commitment."

"No. Population control."

"Other than staying alive, I'm not interested in lifelong anything. We could just..." I scanned down his body to his pants.

He smiled weakly. "The government controls who is given permission to procreate."

"No thanks on that front either."

I had to agree with the Jalvians. Artorians were maybe a little too fanatical in their beliefs, or practices, or whatever they preferred to call them. But did that mean they should be subjugated? Seeker Res would say no. Perhaps, like I'd found with the Jalvians, there were a few assholes among the Artorians, making bad decisions for the rest of them.

Chesser's gaze dipped to his lap where he fiddled with his fingers.

"So all you can do is the head stuff?"

He glanced at me and then away again. "I'm sorry. I should have realized this would be a problem. Too many drinks and there you were with what I needed for my mission. It sure as all hells seemed like you knew what you were doing last night."

"Just followed your lead, actually. I didn't mean to make it sound like I didn't enjoy it. If that's what you've got to offer, I'm fine with that. We were just having fun, right?" I said, hoping to lighten his mood.

"Right." Yet, for agreeing, it didn't sound like he meant it. "Is there anything you'd like me to do? I wouldn't mind learning if you'll show me."

"Maybe later," I said reassuringly.

That moment had passed. If I wanted the chance to talk some Seeker sense into the assholes who were keeping him from enjoying a full sexual experience, we had a job to do. Unless we pulled this off, not a single Artorian other than Chesser would care what I had to say on that matter or any other. They'd be too busy working for their Jalvian overlords.

He eyed my cheek. "I hope last night wasn't too uncomfortable?"

I worked my jaw a little, exploring the discomfort level now that the alcohol had fully worn off. That Jalvian had a solid punch. "It's fine. Kinda used to being sore somewhere at all times. Comes with the job."

"Which one?"

I chuckled. "All of them. Speaking of which, I should shower and get changed before the corridors are full from shift change. Don't leave your suite. Any of you. I mean it."

He nodded, still averting his gaze.

"Watch your suite terminal. I'll contact you as soon as I see anything on the inbound logs. Besides, I should probably go before your crew wakes up. Save you from awkward questions."

"They wouldn't, but thank you for considering it."

Did he often worm his way onto space stations to spy on the enemy and brain-sex his way through compatible women on board? Was he merely using me for his mission? Hell, was I just using *him* for his mission because it might benefit me? Time would tell, I supposed. Vivid memories of the night before assured me that no matter which of us was using the other, there were pleasurable benefits involved.

"I'll be in touch." I walked out of the bedroom to find two of his crew eating at the table between me and the door.

One of them smiled. The other glanced at Chesser's open door and shook his head before returning to his meal. While I would have preferred to give them both the fuck off gesture I knew well in human and Jalvian, I didn't know if they'd understand it, being Artorian. Considering that I might be traveling with them for however long it took to reach Artor, I decided to just ignore them and leave.

When I got back to my suite, I sent Peter a message, wishing him well with his surgery and one to Jenner to let him know I was safe and all was well. The next one made me nervous. I messaged my captain to request a meeting.

By the time I had showered and changed, he had replied with a time and location. I had just long enough before I had to leave to meet him to grab a breakfast bar from my kitchen and eat it methodically while skimming the station news feed.

Since taking my job on the station, the captain had done his best to keep our affiliation quiet. If the Jalvians assumed I was a Jalvian by-blow working security on the station, that served our needs just fine. Not working openly for the Verian military kept them clear of violating any occupation rules set out by the Jalvians. My reporting directly to Parishnev on occasion didn't raise any eyebrows if I was merely security.

Captain Bennat waited for me in Parishnev's office. As usual, he gestured for me to sit while he remained standing. Most Verians took our height differences in stride, but my superior officer had issues with me looming over him. In the interest of a favorable outcome, I sat.

"What's this about assisting Artor?" he asked, getting directly to business. His pale green eyes studied me intently.

I explained Chesser's mission and how it could benefit us by driving Jal to pull its forces from the Verian Cluster.

"You think you could pull this off alone?" he asked incredulously.

"I wouldn't call working with the Artorians on the station and then, if all goes well, the entire Artorian military, working alone."

His flat face held little expression, always making him a challenge to read. Was he annoyed by my snarky reply? Did he understand my point? Did he like me or want me off his list of responsibilities as soon as possible? As with most every other time we met, I had to guess.

"If the Artorians don't pull them entirely out of the Cluster with this knowledge, this may lessen their presence. Even a little relief would be worthwhile, wouldn't it?"

Captain Bennat nodded. "But losing you here is a gamble I'm not sure I want to take."

I hadn't considered that he might not be willing to let me go. Was I prepared to defect? Doing so would put a big black mark on my record and impact my already precarious social standing on Veria Prime.

"I don't have another Seeker to take your place, Anastassia. You're the only one who can covertly gather intel here in the ways that you do."

Seeker. That title didn't belong to me. Hearing it applied to my person brought up a host of hurt and shame. I wasn't good enough in Res' eyes. He'd been a surrogate father to me after my family's passing. He gave me shelter, council, new friends, the promise of a life where I could help people with this odd ability in my head that set me apart from my kind. Among the Verians, telepathy was a special calling. I'd felt like I finally belonged to something bigger than me, that I was important, not just a disregarded assistant to my father and brother. And then Res had pulled me aside, given me a hug, and told me my training was through. He'd given me all he felt safe offering my tainted heart, not certain that I'd use my training for the safety and betterment of the Verian people.

I'd never achieve the rank of Seeker, but I could help them with the years of training I had. Forever an acolyte, I'd be assisting others above me.

"I'm not a Seeker. Please don't call me that," I said, not hiding the bitterness the word conjured.

Contrary to Res' ruling, I was using my gift and training for the safety and betterment of the Verian people, just not in ways that he or any other Seeker would. Maybe the Verians would have been able to stand up to the Jalvian force if they had a few less pure Seekers to do what needed to be done.

"You may not bear the tattoos and robes, Anastassia, but you have the gift and the training," Bennat said reverently.

We'd argued this point before. It wasn't worth doing so again. "As you say," I uttered, quoting the passive dismissal of my mentor.

Bennat nodded, relief clear in his loose stance. Verians didn't like conflict or even disagreement. It made them anxious.

"Will you at least give me clearance to assist Chesser Ta'set in his mission? If we are successful in gaining the intel he was sent for, I will share it with you and we can evaluate further action then?"

"As long as you don't jeopardize your cover to help this Artorian."

"I won't. You know I'm careful."

Bennat snorted. "That's not the word I'd use. But all the same..." He waved a hand in the air. "See what you can learn and we will talk after."

"Thank you."

He held up his hand again. "Before you go, Parishnev would like a word with you."

Wondering if this was a friendly word or what I might have done, I stayed in my seat as Captain Bennat stepped out of the office.

Commander Parishnev, who on a good day, I considered a friend and, on the others, my secondary boss, walked in and sat behind his desk. The stark lighting of his office glared on his ebony skin.

I switched to my native language, a small celebration of being with another human. "What did I do now?"

He let out a deep bellow of laughter. "Nothing exactly. I just wanted to check in with you in light of our Artorian visitors. Rumor has it that you've set yourself up as their personal guard."

"Fucking Kinny."

His dark eyes twinkled with silent laughter.

"A friendly reminder to be safe and watch your back, that's all. I know you're doing important work for Captain Bennat, but your father's spirit would haunt me if I didn't offer a bit of cautionary admonishment."

Parishnev, a single father of twins himself, was closer to my age than my father's, but he'd vowed to keep an eye on me. Likely some private contingency agreement between two fathers that they'd set up over the card games they'd played once a week.

"My back is covered just fine, thank you."

"I'm sure it is, but all the same, if you need anything, you'll let me know?"

"Actually, two things, now that you've so kindly offered. If you could keep your spiteful second off my back for the next couple of days, that would be very helpful. And I'll need to be tailing two likely high-standing Jalvian Generals, so if you could nudge your actual security staff to make that happen, it would save me from forcing my way in."

"No promises on the first request, though I'll mention letting you do your job. Arita is of her own mind, and as much as I've tried to sway her to your favor, she's having none of it."

"I've noticed, but thank you for trying."

The Verian second in command had little love for me. While most Verians considered me a Seeker in some regard or at the very least respected me for my gift, Arita held only disdain. The spiritual, social, and homeopathic guides were in short supply. Some towns didn't have one and the bigger cities were stretched thin for coverage. If I'd been dismissed, despite such a need for Seekers, I must be evil. There were no shades of grey in her mind.

Parishnev had played mediator between us many times since my return to the station after Res had turned me out. I hated making his job tougher, but I'd done all I could to make peace with Arita. It just wasn't happening.

"Anything else?" I asked, caught in an awkward state of taking a friendly farewell and asking to be dismissed.

"The kids wanted to invite you for dinner, but I'm on the midday to midnight shift for the next four days, so maybe next week?"

"I might not be here. Depending on how this Jalvian general thing goes. I may be taking a hiatus from the station and doing some traveling that will be beneficial to us all."

"I'm intrigued." He leaned forward, resting his elbows on the clean desktop. The terminal, in standby mode, lit with the activity on the work surface.

"I'm not currently at liberty to say more than my task involves the Artorians, two incoming generals, and I have Captain Bennat's approval."

"I liked it better when we could talk freely."

"I know. I'm sorry."

The office, with its deep red walls and Verian crafted wooden furniture, had hosted many heart-felt conversations between us. The loss of his wife and losing my family in close succession had drawn us together beyond our previous family friendship.

"You'll let me know before, if you do take a leave?"

"Of course."

"Go on then. I can see you're anxious to get to it. Whatever it is."

I offered him a quick smile and got out of there before I was inclined to give him more of a hint than I should.

A quick walk brought me to the nearest lift, which I took to the docking control center. I stepped out and into a gaggle of Verians bustling around with datapads in their hands and speaking instructions to their headsets. Beyond the roving workers sat a bank of terminals, half of which were occupied by more of the docking crew. I walked past them to peer down through the large thick plaz panel on the floor. Below me, the maintenance crews swarmed over and around an assortment of small vessels. Outside, on the docking rings, more experienced crews were fulfilling work orders on the large ships. Mover units, under the supervision of the warehousing crew, loaded and unloaded freight. They performed a carefully choreographed dance with the maintenance workers as they shuffled supplies onto the large loading lifts that provided access to the ring level.

The dance relaxed me, as it always did, assuring me that despite the chaos on the public levels, station business progressed as it had every other day since we'd moved here when I was six. I didn't remember much of my first years before coming to the Cluster. Most of those vague recollections were of life on my father's research ship where we'd lived between his jobs.

That ship was now docked in a bay on the ring. I hadn't used it since taking my assignment on the station. There were too many memories in those walls to want to spend time there. Whenever I did, I walked out crushed from the inside out, emotions too close to the surface. Those got me in trouble, usually in an altercation of some sort, even with friends. It was better to keep everything locked down. Safer for all involved.

Uris, the day shift docking manager, grinned upon spotting me. "My dear Anastassia Kazan, what can I do for you today?"

The Arminian stood out among the pale, flat-faced Verians with his slightly taller but more delicate stature, pronounced nose, and yellow-brown skin. There were only a few Armin citizens employed on the station. Most of them preferred their homeworld, much like the Verians. Except they very much welcomed trade from other worlds and had a penchant for turning an enviable profit. That alone set the Verian worlds of Prime and Minor against their neighbors within the Cluster.

Good thing the Verians were too peaceful to do anything more than verbally scorn any Arminians they happened across. As such, Uris and I held a similar disdain from Arita Palaz who, by her pinched look and smartly pressed uniform, was on duty and about to let one or both of us know what was on her mind in a loud, shrill voice.

"Brace yourself," I muttered to Uris. "Angry Verian in three... two..."

"What are you two conspiring to do now?" Palaz asked.

"We're simply doing our jobs, just like you." I stepped between her and poor Uris.

"My job is to make sure this station runs smoothly and complies with the rules agreed upon with the Jalvian and Verian governments."

"And my job is to protect Veria Prime and Minor." I nodded over my shoulder. "His is the same as yours. We're all working together, Arita. We're not the enemy. That would be the Jalvian government."

"Don't let General Zhan hear you say that," she hissed. "You're always in the midst of trouble since your return. You're tainted, Anastassia. Evil."

"Fine. Let me get back to doing evil so I can protect this station and your homeworld."

She narrowed her eyes and glared up at me. "What would your kind know of loyalty to a homeworld? You don't even have one."

I shrugged. "We did once. Might still be there. Never cared to look." Stooping lower, I got in her face. "Because I grew up *here*, tied to your homeworld and your people and this station. This is my home and I will do everything I can, just like you will, to keep it safe."

"We are nothing alike. You have no business here. Get out." She pointed to the door behind us.

"Actually, I do." I fished out my datapad from my pocket and pulled up the letter of authorization Captain Bennat had given me upon my posting, allowing me access to all station systems and records pending Parishnev's approval. I'd shoved it in her face numerous times.

Her face went from nearly transparent white to a faint pink, signaling a rise in volume and a darkening of her tone. "I'll be speaking to the commander about this."

"You do that. I just came from his office. Have a nice day."

Fuming, she stalked to the door she'd pointed me toward and left. Thankfully.

"That was about two minutes faster than last time. Nice job." Uris took a seat at one of the open terminals. "So, what do you need?"

"Any records of a Jalvian with the name of Sharta or Nalaton in the last week to today. They're Generals so ships may be in their name if they've been or are here."

"On it."

Records flashed across his vid screen faster than I could read. They kept going and going.

"This may take a while. We've had a lot of Jalvian activity. They're all coming and going. Always. Like General Zhan is using the station to furlough all Jalvian soldiers in the area."

That wasn't surprising. At least the soldiers couldn't get into trouble on the surface.

"Anything I can help with while you're looking?"

He sat back and gave me a pathetic look. "Could you do that thing you do? My neck has been aching for days."

I supposed other elements of my Seeker training also had their uses.

"Sure." I stood behind him while he resumed his search and placed my fingers on his neck, seeking out the tight spots and pressing firmly in alternating motions. After a few minutes, he let out a relieved sigh. I took a step back.

"Don't you move. The search isn't done and neither are you."

I laughed at his feigned command, but resumed the treatment. Once the muscle knots were gone, I moved upward onto his scalp. His hands stilled and his head dropped forward.

"I could stop, since you've stopped."

"By all the gods, you evil woman, you're lulling me to sleep. On the job, no less. Good thing I'm the boss or I'd have to write myself up."

"So sorry." I went to work on his shoulders instead.

He resumed his data search, but the information was moving much slower now.

"How are you still single?" he asked, his voice all soft and malleable.

I leaned forward until my lips were next to his ear. "I'm evil, remember?"

"But in the best ways." Uris leaned his head back against my stomach and gazed up at me. "If begging would change your mind, I'm not above it."

We'd attempted sex once out of curiosity a few years ago. He'd never seen a naked human, and I'd never seen a naked Arminian. Though we shared a similar humor and got along quite well, our bodies were not very compatible. We'd both agreed to bail and remained friends who enjoyed a great amount of innuendo instead.

I drove my fingers deeper into his shoulder muscles. "I'd break you and you know it."

Uris emitted a deep, rumbling purr. "But I'd enjoy every second until you did."

"Maybe, but Parishnev wouldn't forgive me. He relies on you to keep everything in order here."

"For the sake of duty then, I shall have to live alone all my days." He let out a dramatic sigh that I couldn't help but laugh at.

After a wink to confirm that he was teasing, he resumed his search. It was twenty minutes later that his fingers stilled on the terminal. "Here we go. They docked yesterday. I suppose you'll be wanting to know whether those two ventured onto the station and their current location."

"That would be much appreciated." I worked my way up toward his scalp again, starting in behind his ears.

The rest of the docking staff cast Uris envious glances. I'd likely be getting appointment requests for the next few days. If people asked nicely and I was in a good mood, I wasn't opposed to trading services for favors. Seekers didn't take payment, but I wasn't exactly a Seeker and I wasn't exactly charging. The grey area was acceptable to pretty much everyone but Palaz.

"They've each booked a single suite for last night and tonight. I'll relay the locations to your datapad." He switched programs and his fingers danced over the terminal again.

"Tracer information has been transferred to your account as well." He leaned back against me again. "Anything else I can do to keep your hands on me?"

"Sadly for you, we're done here, but thank you for your help."

"Anytime, even if only to watch you put Palaz in her place."

I leaned down close to him again. "If all goes well in the next day or two, I may be taking a short leave. Keep Palaz in line for me while I'm gone."

"Oh, I will." He turned to study me for a moment. "Business, I take it? You have that mischievous look about you."

"Maybe both."

Uris grinned. "May your profits be plentiful be they measured in credits or pleasure."

"Thank you. You too." I gave his shoulders one last squeeze and headed off to find a quiet place with my datapad so I could find out what the generals were up to.

SIX

I took the lift down to my suite and settled into a corner of the couch, legs spread over the rest of it. Safe in my own space, I opened my datapad and pulled up the information Uris had sent.

The two generals had been assigned rooms on the Jalvian level. While that wasn't a surprise, the fact that they were far from each other was. That would make watching both rooms impossible. At least not by myself. Unless I got access to the corridor surveillance vids, but might be more than I wanted to push Parishnev for.

If General Zhan noticed access to the feed for their level had been granted to me, questions would be asked. I wasn't ready to be exposed over this yet. It would also put Parishnev in an awkward position. I could just hear Arita's tirade over that.

Rather than visual real-time data, it would be better to rely on the location trackers Uris had slipped me access to. That was less traceable, but only provided information whenever their ID data was used to access something on the station. I would have to watch for one ID accessing the room of the other or one of the public meeting rooms. Or opening a tab at any of the food establishments or The Sphinx. Unless they just met up in a hallway somewhere for a walk and talked quietly between them. Dammit.

It wasn't like I could ask Chesser to help watch them. I sighed. Who needed sleep?

I sent Chesser a quick message on his suite terminal, letting him know I was on duty and would get back to him if I learned anything of importance. Then I went to my closet and looked for inspiration. Most of my clothing was Verian in nature. The idea was not to stand out when I was doing Captain Bennat's work. I owned a few crew security uniforms for when I took shifts in an official capacity. Usually, I worked part-time unless Parishnev needed me to fill in more. I hoped he wouldn't mind if I blurred the line this one time. If we got the information Chesser promised was out there, it would be worth the risk of pissing off the station commander.

Making quick work of changing into a uniform, I made sure my hair was neatly braided in keeping with staff standards and then grabbed my datapad and set out. With the pad in my hand, and checking it regularly, I did my best to appear as though I was working. I took the lift to the Jalvian level and did a quick check of Sharta and Nalaton's ID uses. Neither had done anything remarkable beyond order food and have a few drinks, but not at the same time as the other. I prayed I hadn't missed any important information exchanges.

Picking Nalaton, solely because his room was closer to the lift, I parked myself within view of his door and opened the nearest access panel. Security should check air filtration systems now and then, shouldn't they?

An hour there started to feel forced, so I moved farther down the corridor to the next panel. The label informed me I was staring at the inner workings of the power grid for this section. Doing my best to not actually touch anything other than the panel, I poked around in there for another hour. Nalaton's door remained sealed.

My datapad beeped softly. General Nalaton was using his ID to access his suite terminal. I hoped it was for something inane, like viewing the vast assortment of Jalvian porn that had inundated our data storage since the occupation, rather than having a private vid call with General Sharta. My nerves tingled as I pondered my options.

What if it *was* a private vid call? What if I was missing the information I was supposed to be overhearing? I groaned. Probing minds without a visual on the person was harder, and doing that without being felt was a skill level I wasn't sure I was at.

Committed to doing something more than poking around behind access panels for another hour, I was securing the first corner of the panel when heavy footsteps brought me to attention.

Having a one on one with our Jalvian overseer was not on my agenda for the day. Staff, visitors, even Jalvians who angered him had a high rate of losing their privileges, jobs, or even lives. I'd helped clean up after more than one unlucky encounter with Zhan since the occupation had begun.

I pasted a pleasant smile on my face. "General Zhan. Is there something I can help you with?"

He regarded me with piercing blue eyes. The array of metals on his

uniform jingled with each expansion of his broad chest. Like many of
the Jalvian officers, he wore his straight blond hair long and tied back
at the nape of his neck.

I kept my mouth shut and did my best to keep my gaze off of Nalaton's door. Just doing my job, nothing more. Nothing to see here.

"What's this all about? Is the station falling apart?" he grumbled.
"Shoddy quality, if you ask me. If it were of Narvan design, we'd all be
more comfortable."

"The station is adequate, sir." Inspiration hit me. "With the Artorians on board, it seemed prudent to check for sabotage. One of them
was seen in this corridor last night."

His gaze narrowed. "Not the one *you* were seen with, I take it?"

"Just keeping an eye on him, sir. Some of your soldiers had too much
to drink. They were violating the treaty and the officers in attendance
had their hands full trying to control them. I thought it best to assist by
keeping the Artorian separated to avoid in any further incidents."

"You weren't being friendly."

"I work for the station, sir. I'm just doing my best to keep everyone
in line."

General Zhan let out a mildly positive sounding grunt. "A Jalvian
bastard will do. Come with me. Time to prove your loyalty."

I followed the tall, imposing general down the hall. Right to Nalaton's door. My heart raced. Was I being exposed?

He palmed the panel and stood stiffly as if counting every second
he was kept waiting. Nalaton wisely didn't keep us in the corridor for
long. He opened the door and waved us inside. I stood in General
Zhan's shadow, trying to take everything in while doing my damnedest
to not look like I was paying attention to my surroundings.

I don't know what I was expecting to see, maybe still frames of
surveillance or detailed plans in writing. There was nothing obvious
in sight beyond the standard furniture and a Jalvian uniform jacket
draped over one of the chairs.

General Nalaton regarded Zahn with a tight nod while casting a
gaze of clear regret to the jacket that was currently not on his person to
illustrate his honors.

"General Sharta will meet us in half an hour. The space has been
confirmed and deemed secure," General Nalaton said.

"Excellent. You will both come alone. I will meet you there. We're
going to do a sweep of our own to verify the security of the space."

Nalaton's upper lip curled. "You don't trust my word?"

"I know this station. You do not. As little Kazan pointed out moments ago, we have Artorians aboard. They would like nothing more than to take us all down with a bit of calculated sabotage."

My mouth went dry. I kept my head down. Getting drafted into Zhan's service, no matter how temporary, was a risk I wasn't comfortable with. But Zhan didn't care about anyone's comfort other than his own. The only redeeming factor was that he was putting me right where I needed to be.

"I would prefer an escort, as previously planned," General Nalaton said.

"You'll draw more attention to yourself. Come alone. We'll go now. Follow in fifteen. Sharta will join in thirty. A staggered arrival will garner less attention," commanded Zhan.

He didn't wait for a confirmed agreement. General Zhan headed out the door, his long legs easily eating up the distance between Nalaton's room and our destination. I followed, taking two steps to each of his.

"Do you know your name of the disgrace who failed to prevent your conception?" he asked over his shoulder.

"No, sir. I do not." I knew firstFhand that Jalvian men were meticulous in their pregnancy prevention outside of their race, but damn, I felt bad for any actual bastards out in the universe.

"Just as well. No one wants a bastard, let alone one showing up on the family doorstep."

"I have no plans to leave the station, sir. My job is here."

He nodded. "Good. Here we are."

Zhan came to a stop in front of one of the small public access meeting rooms. They were available for anyone's use as long as they were booked through the station system. The small panel vid beside the door informed me this one was under Zhan's name for the next two hours. Not Nalaton or Sharta. I wouldn't have found it on my own unless I'd been lucky enough to follow one of the other generals without gaining notice. No one would think anything of General Zhan reserving a room. He did that frequently to meet with station staff or various Jalvians in residence.

He stepped into the room and gestured me inside before closing the door behind us.

"You're wondering why you're here." His eyes drilled into me again.

"Yes, sir."

"Commander Parishnev and many of the station staff call you a Seeker. They use your services."

I forced moisture into my mouth. What had he heard, and where was he going with this? "Verian priests are called Seekers, sir. They provide spiritual and personal counseling, as well as a variety of other services for their communities, such as negotiation and holistic medicine."

"Yes, you were useful in the treaty negotiations."

I nodded hesitantly while internally cursing myself for getting involved with the treaty that now brought me under his notice.

"Do you require a mediator today?"

Zahn stared me down for a silent minute. "Rumor has it that you have some sort of truth-seeing training from the natives?"

"To a degree, yes, but—"

He had a way of filling the room with threat and malice without having to speak. Half of me was deeply envious. The other half was fighting to keep my terror contained.

"Did you use this seeing during our negotiations?"

"No. It wasn't necessary."

"Wasn't it?"

The heavy air of implication hung over me. A ghostly tickle slithered in my mind, the memory of Chesser attempting to probe me. Zahn didn't have that ability, yet my imagination was sure that he did.

I subtly shook out my tense muscles and met his gaze. "Full disclosure, sir, truth-sense works best on Verians. Jalvians have different mannerisms, habits, and social structures. I am not trained in your tells."

He pressed his full lips together, forming a tight line. "You expect me to believe that? Living on a world who fought against us, no matter how briefly? They didn't train you to know your enemy?"

In fact, they hadn't. Verians didn't view anyone as enemies. They merely wanted to be left alone. Seekers should have been sent out to negotiate with the first rounds of raiders, but the Verian people didn't want to risk losing them. Seekers were too rare, too valuable. And now the entire Verian Cluster was under Jalvian control.

I wasn't one of those valuable Seekers. No one was risking me but me, and it wasn't like Zahn was going to let me leave before I helped him. If I could get what Chesser needed and rid the Cluster of Jalvians, that was more valuable than the revered position that Res had denied me.

"You're not my enemy, sir. I'm one of you. At least partly."

He smiled the slightest bit, and for a second, I thought I'd won a reprieve. Then he leaned in close enough that I could feel his hot breath.

"To be one of these priests, you need to have a degree of that mind shit? Like the fucking Artorians?"

I nodded, feeling the hair on the back of my neck stand. This game was getting more dangerous by the second. I'd teased Uris about breaking him due to our size and build differences, but now I was entirely in his place with General Zhan. And I didn't like it.

"One of us." He scoffed. "Fucking abomination. That's what you are. Quit eyeing the door and look at me." He brought his face even closer to mine. "Can you read intentions if you can get in their heads?"

My insides were churning, and I was pretty sure he could smell the sweat seeping into my uniform, but if there was a chance in hell that I could turn this around, I was going to try for it. And to do that, I had to keep my shit together.

"Common policy is we don't get in anyone's head without consent, sir." Not that I followed the policy, but I was going to hang onto it with my last breath to make Zhan believe I wasn't there to skim every Jalvian tidbit I could find.

"Policy." He rolled his eyes and sneered. "I'm sure you're every bit as honorable as the fucking Artorians. But I'll get you your consent. Can you do what I'm asking?"

If he was asking me to read the other generals despite how much he plainly despised the ability to do so, I was inclined to point out the irony. I also wanted to live to leave the room. Biting down on my comment, I nodded instead.

"Yes, I can, sir."

"Good. Do you speak fluent Jalvian?"

"Sorry no. Not much call for it out here until you arrived."

He scowled. "Trade it is then. You'll sit across from me. I want to see your face. Do you understand?"

I nodded again.

"You'll read Generals Nalaton and Sharta and signal me if they are insincere about any statements they make. Their plan seems too good to be true." He shook his head. "They claim they can put the Narvan firmly in our hands, but I'm not ready to commit funds or troops to them until I can be sure what they propose will work. You are going to be that deciding factor, Kazan. I hope you're ready."

I wasn't. Not by a long shot. While his proposal would give me everything Chesser was asking for, I had the creeping feeling that I wouldn't be walking out of the room no matter how many snarky comments I kept to myself or how cooperative I was.

I sat in the chair General Zhan indicated on the other side of the narrow, white plaz table. The smooth surface only amplified the sweat building up on my palms. I moved my hands to my lap, wondering if I could blindly access the datapad in my pocket to contact someone to extract me.

General Zhan remained standing, his attention divided between me and the closed door. If he caught me using my datapad, I'd be dead for sure. I shivered even though I was sweating.

General Nalaton arrived on time. He gave me a curious glance and took a seat at one end of the rectangular table. The beige walls pressed in on me. Though my uniform was a similar tone, I knew I was not blending in with anything. All General Zhan needed was to shoot first and claim I was a spy later. He'd weather whatever censure Parishnev and Captain Bennat could muster to throw at him. My usefulness was limited to two hours. Panic lit in my veins.

How could I contact anyone without using my datapad or bolting out the door? General Nalaton stared me down but didn't ask questions. General Zhan remained standing between the door and the table, tapping one finger on his crossed arms. After five minutes of this silence, I was sure I would burst.

Once General Sharta joined us, we'd get started and my life timer would tick down even faster. Who knew how long their meeting would actually go? It could be fifteen minutes for fuck's sake. I had no intention of joining the countless casualties of their war.

I tried to take a full breath and think calmly. The only reason I was in this room was because both sides were using my telepathic gift. Maybe it would also save me.

Verian Seekers needed to be near to touching to use their gift, but I didn't. I'd always worked within my line of sight, in the same room, but maybe I was limiting myself. If Jalvians were so concerned that their enemy could read their thoughts and invade their heads, talking at a distance had to be possible.

In the hopes I was more like Artorians than Verians, I sought out the mind I'd thoroughly enjoyed intertwining with the night before. Opening myself to the barrage of thoughts between me and Chesser, I spent precious minutes casting about without direction. Then, like a beacon, his anxiety and frustration stood out among all the others. I'd been in his mind. We'd mentally touched. I knew him.

Latching on to that connection, I allowed myself a few seconds to level out my breathing so I could concentrate properly.

"Can you hear me?" I asked in his mind.

"Anastassia?"

"I'm in that meeting you wanted, but I don't think I'll get out of it. I need you to go to the station clinic and find Peter Strauss, the man I was with at The Sphinx last night before I sat with you. Do you remember him?"

"Enough, I think. Why?"

"Peter knows what I do here and can get you to Parishnev, the station commander. Parishnev can pull in Captain Bennat. Between the two of them, they will hopefully be able to work something out to extract me from General Zhan's private meeting in conference six."

"Got it. Peter, commander, captain, extract from six."

If he worked too efficiently, I might get nothing of value. I'd come too far to walk away with nothing when the plans Chesser needed were so tangible.

"Convince them to remain outside the room until I tell you. You need to stay out of Zhan's sight or you won't be leaving either."

"Understood. Be safe."

"Bit late for that."

I closed our connection, solidifying it for use later. Once the meeting was wrapping up, I wouldn't have time to hunt Chesser's mind down again.

General Sharta arrived. He took his spot at the other end of the table.

Knowing I had a plan in motion, whether it would pan out or not, alleviated a fraction of my anxiety. I still would have given every credit I owned to be standing outside the door. Taking the chance at getting caught skimming thoughts but having room to run beat actually sitting in the room with three large, armed generals. I hoped to hell this would be worth it.

SEVEN

"You're wondering why the little bastard is here," General Zhan stated. "The Verians have trained her in their way of seeing truth. We will continue Trade and you will allow her to do as I have asked or you will not receive the funding or troops you ask for. Is that understood?"

Nalaton and Sharta nodded, watching me warily. At least he hadn't called me an abomination in front of them. As it was, my chances of surviving the prejudices of all three Jalvians were in the negative.

General Zhan finally took his seat across from me. "Now then, what is this about ending the war for good?"

With my nerves as scattered as they were, it took me a few minutes to get into the proper mindset to delicately reach out to Nalaton and then Sharta's mind. Being in two minds at once was disorienting, especially considering the hate-filled images flooding both of their heads.

Some of that hate was aimed at me. My unknown abilities lumped me in with Artorians. Artorians were the enemy. They needed to be subjugated, reined in, brought to heel. Made submissive.

Sharta had explicitly graphic thoughts on how that should go with me. My cheeks burned despite my efforts to keep what I was seeing to myself.

"It's more than reading physical tells, isn't it, little bastard?" General Zhan stretched out in his seat, placing a weapon I'd only seen once before on the table. One hand remained on the pulse pistol, a single finger slowly tapping the barrel.

If he fired that, there wouldn't be enough of me left for Peter to put back together. The cleaning crew would be wiping me off what was left of the wall.

I kept my head down, but my eyes refused to leave the pulse pistol.

"I'm only doing what you've asked."

Zhan nodded but appeared no more tolerant of me than before.

Sharta cleared his throat and rested his arms on the table. "Our forces have been building near Syless, out of sight. We've been keeping the Artorian fleets busy defending Artor and Karin. If you join us, the forces here in the Cluster will be enough to conquer Moriek once and for all, cutting Artor and Karin off from their additional resources."

General Nalaton pulled a datapad from his jacket pocket and set up a projection map so we could all see. "We've simulated the proposed action."

Tiny worlds came to life in full color before me. Despite trying to stay in their minds, I was utterly distracted by the battle taking place above the table.

A blue and green world surrounded by a spinning layer of golden satellites grew larger than the rest. Ships marked with a blue glimmer gathered all at once just above the satellite shield, streaming in from a nearby world with a swirling, murky grey atmosphere. I assumed it must be Syless. While ships lit with an orange glimmer approached, another wave of Jalvian ships burst from a jump gate and streamed to Moriek to create an overwhelming force.

The blue ships easily overwhelmed the orange fleet, obliterating them until nothing but wreckage remained. Satisfaction and ruthless glee flowed from both Nalaton and Sharta, reminding me I was still touching their thoughts.

"Once their fleet is halved, they'll fall back to Artor, leaving Karin exposed. We'll have them right where we've always wanted. On their knees," boasted Sharta.

"Where did you get the resources to build these additional ships? Syless is nothing but a wasteland of sand, a fucking consolation offering from the Artorians during our expansion," said General Zhan.

"We've been commandeering trade vessels, supply ships bound for Artor and other worlds outside the Narvan. Resources that would have gone to reinforcing their fleets have instead gone to ours," Nalaton said.

While his voice exuded pride. Trepidation edged his thoughts. I dug deeper. Nalaton fought me every step of the way. Wrestling mentally was draining and made me nauseous.

Maybe I could talk my way out of this room and leave my alliances out of it. I shook my head and did my best to keep the contents of my stomach from rising to my throat.

That caught General Zhan's attention. "Speak the truth of it."

If I could deflect that pistol toward someone else, I might live to leave. There was enough truth in what I'd seen to guess at a little more to really drive Zhan mad.

"General Nalaton has been skimming resources meant for Jal to build up his own fleet on Syless. He's been bribing supply ships. He hopes to be seen as the hero and gain favor for his name for generations."

Sharta pounded on the table. "No matter. We have the ships. We can take control of this war and win once and for all."

General Zhan pried his fury-filled gaze from Nalaton to Sharta. "And what of the troops on Moriek? Will they go peacefully so that we need not divide our forces to hold one world while we take the next? What about the satellite net? If that is damaged, Moriek will revert to its dim, muddy origins and be of little use to us within a generation."

Sharta's bravado wavered but didn't disintegrate. "A small force will remain to fully subdue Artorian ground forces, but most of the combined fleet can move on to Karin. As for the satellites, our ships will need to be mindful of them. Preservation of the prize is a priority."

General Zhan stared me down.

"Truth."

He nodded, returning his attention to Sharta. "And you're sure Artor doesn't have additional ships in reserve, as we do here?"

"If they did, they would have pulled them by now. They're on the defensive. We only need to form a fist and squeeze."

General Sharta's thoughts raced with excitement, envisioning a host of dark-skinned men and women on their knees as he executed them all. Chesser could have been one of them.

Were Artorians any better than the Jalvians in the room? I didn't know for sure. What I did know was what the Jalvians had done to take Veria Prime and Minor, and how they treated the citizens on the station I called home. I might be jumping into bed with an enemy just as bad, but if I could endear myself to the Artorians like I was doing with Chesser... If I took this information to his superiors instead of just handing it over, I might have a say in how they moved forward. I might be able to protect the Cluster and keep their deadly bickering contained in the Narvan.

Zahn again turned to me. I nodded.

"Show it again," he commanded Nalaton.

Eager to have negative attention off himself, Nalaton again activated the datapad and restarted the projected simulation.

We all watched as Jalvian forces obliterated the Artorian fleet, as Moriek took on a blue glow. A smaller world, a moon, I realized, was surrounded and turned blue. A ragged fleet vainly attempted to protect a vast world, vibrant with the colors of teeming life under an organized web of satellites. Weapons fired from the web and the orange ships, but they were not enough. As the action raced by in simulated time, they all fell or were taken. Everything in the projection took on a blue shimmer.

Excitement filled the small space.

"What do you say, Kazan? Is this true? Will it come to pass?" General Zhan asked.

What list of skills were Seekers rumored to have? "I can't see the future."

He picked up the pulse pistol.

"Now!" I shouted in Chesser's head, praying he'd found someone to extract me and that he was outside the door. I'd been too wrapped up in what was going on in the room to check in with him, and he'd been silent.

"Just as well, or you would never have come into this room."

I stared at the pistol being aimed at me, my breath caught in my throat.

A split second later, he spun to Nalaton and fired. The energy blast was invisible but intense. The thrust of the beam shoved me sideways out of my chair. It was as if all the air in the room smashed into me. I fell to the floor, gasping.

Nalaton also fell to the floor. His body hit the carpet, empty eyes wide with surprise, his mouth gaping in a silent scream. His chest had caved in as though his bones had dissolved. Blood seeped through his jacket, staining the patches and medals until they were an indistinguishable mess. The chair was in tatters, pieces embedded in the wall and littering the floor.

An insistent knock on the door registered in my pounding ears. Everything seemed to be in slow motion, distant.

I'd gotten as far as my knees, grasping the table with trembling fingers, when Parishnev burst in with Captain Bennat on his heels.

Bennat took one look at me and then focused his attention on General Zhan, keeping his face entirely neutral. "Are you safe, General? We were investigating possible Artorian sabotage in the area when the walls shook. Was there a bomb?"

"All is well," Zhan said confidently, putting his pistol away. "Sorry about the wall and the mess."

General Sharta stared at the opposite end of the table where Nalaton had been. He remained in his seat.

"I think we're done here," said Zhan, turning to General Sharta.

"You'll get your funding and troops. We'll be in contact."

"Thank you," he said with only a slight tremor. Sharta stood and ducked past Parishnev and Bennat to escape the room.

"Kazan, I believe you have duties elsewhere?" Bennat gave me a disdain-filled dismissive glance.

I hoped it was an act, but regardless, I took my scattered wits from the room of carnage with great haste. Parishnev followed me.

"Get to your suite and stay there. I'll post a guard," he ordered.

"I can't stay, not after what I've seen."

Zhan certainly wouldn't want other Jalvians to know he'd used my services. Sharta would keep quiet because he wanted his place at Zhan's side, but I was a loose end. "Zhan will take care of me no matter what guards you post. He has his ways."

More than a couple of bodies had turned up since his residency, some Jalvian, some local. None of them looked like what remained of Nalaton, but they were just as dead.

We hadn't made it out of sight before Zhan and Bennat exited the room. Parishnev shared a split second of regret before shoving me against the wall and boxing me in with his thick arms. He began berating me for trying to endear myself to General Zhan when I was supposed to be part of his crew and doing my job.

Again, I hoped it was an act, but he was very convincing. After Zhan had passed, Parishnev continued his rant another minute until Zhan was long out of sight. Only then did he drop his arms. With his angry words pummeling my thoughts, I made my near-running escape to the lift, praying no one else would be in it.

As luck would have it, a crowd of Verians and assorted races of station visitors filled the space, leaving me just enough room to squeeze in. New ships must have docked, expelling their crews to enjoy the station or make trade deals. Uris was probably busy dealing with those reports.

Peter...but what help could he offer? He was a doctor, not versed in hiding or protecting the knowledge in my head from Zhan. The more my thoughts spun, I didn't feel safe going to any of my friends. That would lead them into Zhan's sights if he thought I'd shared what I'd seen with them.

A handful of the other occupants in the lift jostled me as they moved past to get off on the next floor. While that left more room, my skin was crawling. The disdain in Bennat's gaze was burned into my brain. I could smell Parishnev's early lunch on his breath as he yelled in my face.

My heart raced, and my breath came in gasps. Nothing felt safe anywhere. My back itched like Zhan still had his pistol aimed at me. He could look up my suite location. As station overseer, he had access to the public databases. If he was willing to nonchalantly kill one of his own, he could also eliminate the Artorians. Who was going to stop him? Who was he accountable to? From the way Nalaton and Sharta acted, they might all have been the same rank, but he was their superior. Was he hanging back here in the Cluster to observe the Narvan and pull strings from afar?

We needed to prod him from his safe place and put him somewhere he could be removed. He needed to go back to the Narvan where Chesser's people could take care of him.

Chesser. We had to get off the station. Immediately.

EIGHT

I exited the lift on the next floor and hurried to the suite Chesser shared with his crew. Pressing my sweaty palm to the access panel, I waited, shifting from foot to foot.

The moment the door opened, I darted inside, not caring which of the Artorians might be waiting. As it turned out, it was all of them. Chesser surged forward and grabbed my shoulders. I didn't want to look at him. Not at anyone. My senses were overwhelmed and my wits scattered to the opposite ends of the station. I needed to sit, to close my eyes, to take a breath.

"Anastassia." He shook me gently. "Did you get it?"

I nodded. "We have to go. Now. Zhan won't wait."

"Wait for what? How soon is he leaving?"

"No. He'll kill me. I need to go. Right now."

Chesser raked a hand through his short hair and grimaced. "Getting the information was the first part of the plan. We haven't figured out the rest. If we leave now, they'll pick us off as soon as we're off the station. You saw our ship. We barely made it here. Repairs aren't done yet. If any of the Generals leave before us, we'll have no chance to beat them back to Narvan. The plans will be useless."

Through the chaos in my head, thoughts organized themselves into an orderly plan of action.

A calm voice that sounded like mine but surely couldn't be considering the chaos dancing just outside that plan, ordered Chesser and his men to grab what they needed. None of them moved.

"Now!" I yelled. My nerves shot electric jolts through my limbs, making it impossible to stand still.

They scattered, running into the bedrooms and through the suite, gathering up everything they'd brought. The Artorians quickly reassembled, eyeing me uncertainly.

"Your ship will remain here. We'll take mine. Give me a minute with your terminal."

I turned my back on them and requested a connection to Uris. After a hurried conversation to get my ship up to any available dock, I took Uris up on his offer to make sure it was fully stocked and fueled. Then we moved on to keeping the Artorian suite assignment open for several more days and his promise to falsify records showing meals being ordered to the suite.

"You'll be careful?" Uris asked, concern contorting his delicate features.

"I'll do my best. You better be too. This ruse won't last long, and General Zhan won't be happy with anyone who helped us escape. Parishnev will be forced to go along with whatever he decrees."

Uris nodded solemnly. "I've had other job offers. Perhaps it's time I take one of them. I'll miss your hands, evil woman."

"I'll miss your knotty neck." It was one thing to blow my cover here and jeopardize my job, but losing Uris on top of the shit Bennat and Parishnev had already heaped on me was hard to stomach. "I..."

Uris nodded. "I know. You too." He ended the call.

I swallowed past the lump in my throat, unsure of what I'd been going to say but grateful Uris knew me well enough to guess. Expressing feelings had never been my strong point. The next call wouldn't be any easier, but at least I hadn't burned Peter's job.

Worry lined his thin face. "What did you get yourself into, Anastassia?"

"Nothing good. Well, maybe it is, but I have to leave."

"I heard there was trouble. One hears about shattered bodies in the clinic."

"It was a Jalvian."

"I also heard you were a witness to that."

"Which is why I'll be back if I can clear the station of Jalvians. It won't be safe for me until I do. Keep my suite secure, will you?"

He nodded solemnly. "Your family will be safe under my watch."

I took a shuddering breath and closed the connection. The few small hints I'd kept of my father and brother were in my suite and on the ship we were about to take.

Last night, when I'd considered taking a brief trip with Chesser, it had seemed like an adventure. The reality of having to flee my home because I'd been witness to a murder and classified war plans was far grimmer.

"Let's go. Keep your heads down and attempt to mix with any of the new non-Verian crews moving about the corridors."

The four men followed close behind as we left their suite and headed the opposite way from which I'd come.

"The lift is this way," Chesser said beside me.

"There's a smaller, staff-only one, and if that's occupied, we'll take the stair tube. The fewer people who see us, the better."

That would have all been well and good on most days, but with the influx of visitors, the corridors of the general housing level were awash with bodies.

We wove our way through the fray, moving steadily toward the staff lift. Arita Palaz stood between me and our destination, her hands on her hips and a scowl set on her flat face.

"Commander Parishnev would like a word with you."

"He already shared plenty of them." I considered elbowing my way past her, but that would only create a scene that would attract attention.

"And rightly so. I don't know what you're up to, Kazan, but Bennat's letter won't get you out of this one. He's waiting to speak to you."

"Tell him it's what we talked about, and that I'll do my best to uphold my end of the deal."

She laughed. "You think I'm letting you go?" Palaz pulled her stunner and aimed it at me.

Well fuck. As anathema as the misuse of my gift might be, what I was about to do was for the good of every non-Jalvian on the station and the four men with me. I dove into her mind, probing deeply enough that I could disrupt her thoughts and control over her body. The effort it took to do so wiped out what little energy I had left after playing truthsayer for General Zhan.

Arita's stunner fell to the floor. She staggered one direction. I staggered the other, waiving for the Artorians to follow me. We left Arita clutching her head and leaning against the wall. We hurried to the lift access.

I used my code to open the door, and once it closed and we were on our way to the docking ring, assumed the same position in which we'd left Arita.

Chesser's hand again rested on my shoulder.

"I'll live," I assured him as much as myself.

The lift door opened to an offshoot corridor near the docking control room where I'd been earlier. Thoughts of Uris and everyone else I was leaving behind rushed in on me. As did the chaos I'd be causing by taking the Artorians off the station. I could leave them to their own ship and luck. If I was feeling generous, I could even offer them my ship, so they'd have a better chance. But that would still leave me to run from Zhan.

I drew a ragged breath. There was no easy fix to this and more to gain by leaving.

"Anastassia."

I became aware of Chesser's lips hovering near my ear and that I'd stopped, my body and mind begging for a few minutes to take everything in.

"Yes, we need to keep moving." I forced myself to stand up straight and put one foot in front of the other. I led the way to the extension where Uris had said my ship would be waiting.

Two human members of the docking ring staff were exiting when we arrived. I didn't recognize them, but they both wore friendly smiles.

One leaned in close, speaking our native language, "Uris wishes you luck. We all do. We pray you can deliver."

"Thank you."

I didn't know how much they knew or exactly what Uris had implied I was delivering, but as long as they weren't standing in my way, I'd take all the well wishes I could get. We needed them.

I walked onboard. The Artorians followed.

The filtered air smelled exactly as I remembered, bringing a wash of fond memories. I vividly recalled my father smiling from the control panel as we set off to another site or world to study plants, soil, or mingle with the farmers there to learn their secrets. We'd been on a mission of prosperity, to share knowledge so that everyone could be self-sustaining and healthy with their own food supply.

Now the ship was filled with nervous, hulking Artorians. Instead of gathering farming secrets, I was using the family ship to race off to the Narvan with stolen intel that might change the fate of entire worlds. I supposed that was still a mission of sharing knowledge, but I didn't remember my father ever looking as scattered and afraid as I was just then.

"There's a cargo hold in the back. Set up there. It should be a smooth ride to the jump gate, assuming we don't get discovered and blown to bits." I pointed them toward the rear of the ship, past the three bedrooms and the tiny kitchen where the table had doubled as my father's office between meals.

I only flew the ship a few times a year, and those trips were between the surface of Veria Prime and the station. Having watched my father and sometimes my brother, who would let me help, I had a solid grasp of how to pilot the ship. My solo flights had helped shore up my knowledge, but I was, by no means, an expert. The ship wasn't armed beyond a few turrets that were all controlled from the main panel where I stood. I'd watched my father use them to break up a debris field once, but I'd never used them. We wouldn't stand a chance if General Zhan came after us.

Chesser reemerged from the cargo hold. "They're settled. What can I help with?"

"Staying out of sight when I need to speak to the Jalvians guarding the jump gate?" I smiled weakly.

"Right. Anything before that?"

A hug seemed like a stupid thing to ask for at the moment, considering we didn't know each other all that well and that I needed to be focused on my flight check. Yet that was the answer on the tip of my tongue.

It was a weak request and I couldn't afford that in front of Chesser right now. I stuck with a half-assed smile and a shake of my head.

Chesser glanced around. While I went about re-familiarizing myself with the controls and getting the ship prepared to release from the docking clamps, he settled his large frame into the chair against the wall that I'd used for the same purpose when my father stood where I was now. It offered a good view of the large vid projection of our surroundings and the pilot and what they were doing without being underfoot or visible in any projection conversations. My brother had called it my shadow chair. He'd always joked that I was lurking. In fact, I'd just wanted to be included, but they were a tight duo and I'd been too young to get in on their partnership before it had solidified. Their work had left little room for me.

My head throbbed and my hands shook, but I kept breathing steadily, forcing myself to stay on my feet, to let my memories of what I needed to do run on autopilot. To not think too much about Nalaton's terror-filled face on the floor or the barrel of Zhan's pulse pistol staring me down.

Breathe. In and out. Repeat.

Mostly confident I had everything in order, I put in the request for docking release. Moments later, a tremor passed through the ship along with a heavy metallic clang. The docking clamps released.

The clear for takeoff message flashed on the docking relay. I input the recommended flight path to clear station space and then allowed myself to sink into the tall stool at the controls. There was nothing to be done but hang on until I could enter the next flight commands.

"Anastassia? Do you want to talk about it? What you saw or heard?" Chesser asked.

Did I want to give him the information he'd asked for? No. No, I did not. It was my bargaining chip, not his to turn in for a fat reward.

I shook my head and kept my eyes on the control panel.

If I gave it all to him, he now had my ship. He could get home and wouldn't need me at all. I'd already survived being a snipped loose end once today. I wasn't about to offer my neck again.

The station fell away on the vid view. My home with my friends, the people I cared about and who cared about me. Except Palaz, she could rot. I hoped she had just as much of a headache as I did.

I rubbed my eyes and then pressed my hands to my temples. If only I had time to visit a Seeker for some relief. Practicing the arts upon oneself wasn't very effective.

The flight path indicator dinged, alerting me to enter the next destination.

Chesser let out a loud, relieved sigh. "Well, it seems we've escaped the station."

"We've still got the gate. Don't celebrate yet."

He nodded, but smiled. "Thank you for this, Anastassia. Once we get those plans home, you can return and go back to what you were doing before I put all this on you."

I noticed the distinct lack of mention of his earlier offer to join his team as a freelance agent. Had that been only to manipulate me? An enticement?

"I don't think it will be so simple as that. I may have burned some big bridges by helping you."

"Your captain? The commander?" Chesser shook his head. "Your doctor friend insisted I speak to them myself, to explain what we were up to. They're behind you. Behind us."

"It sure didn't sound like it when they came for me."

He unfolded himself from the chair. It was the right size for me, for a human, but a cramped perch for him. Chesser rose and, after a noticeable check of the vid and controls, wrapped his arms around me, pulling me onto his chest. I kept my relieved sigh to myself.

My forehead rested on his shoulder.

I wasn't sure how I felt about that, having been the tall one in the room most of my life, towering over the Verians and Arminians. Being considered short among Jalvians was disconcerting and now Artorians too. I was headed to the Narvan, which was filled with people his size. But he was warm and comforting and talking, I realized, as I again shook off the daze.

"It's been a rough day," I mumbled against his shoulder.

"They were worried about you. Both of them. And quite displeased that I'd put you in a position of General Zhan's direct focus."

I could see that, Parishnev especially. He took his promise to my father seriously. Bennat knew I took risks, sometimes larger ones than he preferred, but they usually paid off. He knew that too.

"If they were harsh with you, it was for their own protection. For yours as well."

A glimmer lit in me, the promise that I might be able to return with a minimum of apologies once the Jalvians were gone. "I hope so."

If I stayed in his embrace much longer, I would fall apart. I needed to keep myself together. To get all of us to his homeworld. To get to know him before I decided whether I could expose genuine emotions, or if we were just mutually using each other while enjoying sexual benefits.

I peeled myself off of him. Regretfully, I admitted once I'd returned to my task of entering the flight path to the jump gate. The controls didn't offer the solid reassurance his body did. But I knew what had to be done. The jump gate coordinates were already in the system, as were the coordinates to get routed to the Narvan, since the ship had been there before.

Chesser stayed by my side, not touching me, but close enough I could feel his warm breath on the back of my neck. After a few silent minutes, he excused himself to go check on his crew.

The room felt empty without his large presence. There was something between us that wasn't there when I was with a Jalvian man and definitely not a human one. I'd never found them very fulfilling.

Maybe it was what Chesser and I had shared mind to mind. I'd had my fair share of fun with many partners, but this one was quickly getting under my skin. Maybe it was something more, something deeper than I'd allowed myself with the others.

Almost as if he'd known I was missing him, Chesser returned to the room and took up his seat in my chair by the wall.

"All good?" I asked, needing to hear his voice, a stable force in the vast uncertainty that was my immediate future.

"Eager to get home, but yes."

With five hours between us and the jump gate, there was nothing for me to do except feel deflated. I was exhausted and weary on levels that had nothing to do with the physical pain I was in from the pulse blast that had killed Nalaton.

"Can you monitor this? Wake me if we're hailed. Don't answer under any circumstances."

He nodded.

"I'm fine," I stated firmly as I walked past him to the second small bedroom that was mine.

"That's what you said last night after getting clocked by that Jalvian." He chuckled softly. "Is that your default setting?"

I shrugged. "You'll know if I'm not. I'll either be biting your head off or unconscious on the floor."

"Noted." He grinned and shook his head. "Get some sleep."

Being alone wasn't in my default settings. Cast adrift from all I'd known, Chesser was the one person I was going to have to depend on other than myself. Assuming we survived the jump gate transfer, we would have three days to get to know one another in close confines with his crew before we reached the edge of Narvan space. Before we were close enough that I had to make the call of where my life would go from here.

Option one was to deliver the plans myself in the hopes I could bargain to get the Jalvians out of the Cluster. Option two was trusting the Artorians to meet my conditions, turning over the plans via transmission once we were in range, and dropping the Artorians off at the first habitable stop. They both ended with heading back home to see about salvaging my life. How fast I got to that depended on Chesser.

I remembered how safe I'd felt with him at my back in bed the night before and wanted that now. I hurt everywhere. Wanting a little comfort was acceptable, wasn't it? Except if he was in there with me, his three men would have free range of my ship. I didn't know them. Not like I knew Chesser, for all the one day of grace that gave him. With a heavy sigh, I went into my room and crawled into bed alone.

The aches in my body were much worse when I came awake to Chesser shaking my shoulder. I groaned and pried my eyes open.

"We're about half an hour out from the jump gate. Thought you might like a bit of time to wake up first."

"Thanks."

He held out a tiny white pill. "Try this. It will make you feel better."

"What is it?" Taking random medication from Peter was one thing. I trusted him. He was also human. "Is it safe for me?"

"A stim. It should be as long as you only take one. We're not that different."

Peter had done a lot of exams on Jalvians since they'd occupied our station. He'd marveled at their similar genetics and also their differences, mostly in body chemistry. The basic structures were fairly similar. Artorians were much like Jalvians, divided by abilities, coloring, social structures and politics. Two halves of one race, Peter had remarked.

Eager for any relief and considering the day ahead and those after it, I took the pill from his hand, summoned up some salvia, and swallowed it.

"We raided the food stores. I hope you don't mind."

"I didn't expect you to go hungry until we reached Artor."

Chesser offered me his hand to help me out of the bed. "We saved you some. Mox made his famous spicy noodles."

I couldn't cook a damned thing, so if his men could, I was all for it. The little kitchen hadn't smelled so good in years. There wasn't room for five of us with the table, chairs, and the food prep and storage space. His crew got up and headed back to the cargo hold, leaving us alone. Chesser heated the plate of noodles and set it in front of me. Steam washed over my face. The glorious smell made my mouth water. Without further invitation, I dug in.

After devouring the delicious noodles in minutes, I put the plate in the cleaner and went back to the pilot station at the front of the ship.

The distant gate was visible on the vid display. Three ships hovered nearby, also visible from our location. One was posted right beside the gate. The others at extended distances before and after it. We'd be in communications range in minutes.

Rethinking my plan, I hurried back to my bedroom and changed into unaffiliated clothing. This was a family research vessel, not associated with any planet or race. We were human, after all, roaming and freelance was our stereotypical role in the scheme of the known universe.

I'd just made it back to my stool at the panel when the stim kicked in. Abundant energy surged through my aching muscles. Though they still hurt, it was much easier to ignore.

"Identify yourself," commanded a stern female Jalvian face from the communication projection.

I calmly relayed my name and ship ID.

"Destination?"

"Frique in the Narvan system. Visiting friends and doing research."

"On Frique?" She shook her head. "Bunch of backwoods farmers and piles of prantha dung."

"Actually, I'm studying the dung. It's essential to understanding how food sources affect the flavor of the meat." I launched into a boring as hell explanation my father had lectured me on when I'd complained about having to gather said dung during one of our studies there.

The woman waved me to silence. "Cargo?"

"Just me and research supplies. I could bring some prantha steaks if I come back this way. If you'd like?"

The woman scowled. "We're showing five life signatures on your ship."

"Research supplies. I have four young prantha that I'm returning to Frique. We tried to introduce them to Veria Prime, but they're not flourishing. Getting skinnier by the day. I'd really hoped they'd take. Your soldiers on the Verian station would have liked a nearby supply of fresh meat."

"Fucking humans, always trying to make a few credits off of everyone else," she grumbled. "Can you prove that you have prantha on board?"

"Do you want me to bring one of the feeble creatures from the cargo hold in here so you can see it?" I scowled. "My living space will smell like dung for days. They're sick. Their dung is currently liquid. Twice as pungent as healthy prantha."

For all her disdain of Frique, she must have been familiar with it because she scowled as if she knew the smell well.

"No one needs that." She grimaced. "Submit your flight plan for approval and hold your position. You'll be notified of your approval status shortly."

I did as she asked, not acknowledging Chesser, even though I could feel him watching me.

Though I was doing my best to remain calm and collected, the stim was making me jittery and my brain was off and running with the fear that every minute we sat here waiting for approval, a ship from the station could arrive right behind us. I prayed Parishnev was still in my corner as Chesser had assured me. As long as he kept Arita's ranting about my attacking her under wraps, General Zhan hopefully wouldn't know that I'd left the station. If he did, he would surely send someone after me.

Minutes ticked by and though the communication projection remained static, I stayed silent and did nothing more than spend the time attending to my cuticles like I had nothing more important to be doing.

When the panel pinged to inform me that another ship was gaining behind us, my stomach dropped to the floor. I didn't have to look at Chesser to know his tension was spiking just as much as my own.

The Jalvian female face reanimated. "Your clearance has been approved. Please enter the gate immediately so we can make room for General Sharta. I'm sure he would appreciate some authentic prantha steaks on Syless if you're looking to deal once you get to Frique."

"Thanks for the lead." I signed off and sped to the jump gate before General Sharta had time to chat with the gate authority about where my ship had come from or that I was human and traveling to the Narvan.

As we passed through the gate, the disorientation of the jump made me shudder. We came out the other side to find another Jalvian ship waiting. My stomach didn't get a chance to settle before another face greeted me on my communication projection.

I relayed our approval status and ID. They verified it and sent us on our way. It wasn't until a good ten minutes later with the gate behind us that Chesser let out a whoop and jumped out of the chair to hug me.

"Sickly prantha." He laughed.

As much as I enjoyed his arms around me, I needed assurances. I stepped back. "You better not be as full of shit as those imaginary prantha. I need those Jalvians off my station."

"I promise I'll do everything I can to make that happen, but if General Sharta is right behind us, we need to get to Artor as fast as possible."

"We'll have to maintain our current course to Frique for another hour before we fall off their long-range scans. I don't want to give anyone a reason to look at us twice. We'd only last seconds in this ship. It's basically defenseless."

"Unlike its pilot." He leaned in to squeeze me again.

I quite liked the feel of that and did not banish him back to his chair as we spent the next hour arm in arm, anxiously watching the vid and controls for any signs of being followed.

When none came, I sagged against him despite the buzz of the stim.

"Sit." He nudged me to the stool. "I'll enter the coordinates to Artor, if you don't mind?"

"Go ahead." It wasn't like I knew where we were going or who we needed to talk to. Now was the time for him to start earning trust.

Once he'd entered the new flight path, he studied the controls. He remarked about the differences of the tech from his own. I gave him what little background I knew of my father's ship, which wasn't much. He'd bought it off of someone before I'd been born, back when my mother was alive. She'd walked these floors with me in her stomach and then died bringing me into the universe. My father had never forgiven me for that.

As the hours passed, Mox prepared another meal, and we took

turns filling the kitchen to eat it. While Chesser's men were friendly enough, they didn't speak much Trade. I enjoyed listening to them speak their own language together. The lyrical quality of it was quite beautiful even if I didn't understand its meaning.

Chesser noticed that I wasn't taking part in the conversation he was having with Mox. He switched to Trade. "Do you speak much Jalvian? The root language is the same."

"Other than cursing? No, not a lot. My tutor was not a happy man."

"Got it. We have a couple of days. I could teach you. If you want?"

"I'm not very good at picking up languages, but you're welcome to try."

"Challenge accepted." He grinned and picked up his fork, repeating a word several times.

I tried to duplicate it, but my tongue couldn't wrap itself around the pronunciation. Mox groaned at my efforts and shook his head. He said something to Chesser and left us alone.

"What did he say?"

"I'd have better luck teaching the fork."

I laughed. "He's right."

By the time we'd finished our meal, I'd pronounced fork and plate right a few times but slaughtered every other word. Chesser called off our lesson to rethink whether he was actually up to the challenge.

He went back to talk to his men for a while and then rejoined me at the control panel. He stood with plenty of space between us and his hands flat on the surface before him.

"Can you tell me what you saw? If General Sharta is close behind, we may not have time to get you to Artor to relay your findings in person. We should transmit them in the morning when we're close enough to open a secure channel."

"General Sharta is heading to Syless, which is beyond Artor, correct?"

He nodded hesitantly.

"Then we will have time to reach Artor."

"Anastassia. Please."

His pleading tone chipped away at my resolve.

"We will relay a message with the loose plan in the morning. Your people will not be caught by surprise. They can get the details when I get there."

"Can I convince you to give me more?"

"You're welcome to try, but in fair warning, I'm much better at fighting with Jalvians than speaking the language."

"I have no interest in fighting you. I saw how you handled yourself. Quite adequately, I must admit."

"Adequately?" I huffed. "If you're not insinuating that you're going to beat it out of me, what did you have in mind?"

He watched the exterior vid view for a few silent minutes, his jaw muscles rippling as if he were working through what was going to say. I let him be while I checked our progress and made a few small adjustments.

"I understand your reservations," he said at last. "You know Jalvian ways. You don't know ours." He licked his lips. "While I was stuck in my room, I did some research on Verian Seekers. They help people get along, right? Social harmony or something like that?"

He'd been using his time wisely. Then again, if his people had sent him specifically, he had to be good at his job and that was getting information.

Much like mine.

I had to give the man credit for appealing to my Seeker training. "Yes."

"Give me today to show you who we are and then you can decide how much information you're willing to send ahead."

"Challenge accepted."

His lips curved into a charming smile that made my toes curl. Good at his job, indeed.

We spent the rest of the day over the projection console. He pulled up everything my ship's database had on the Narvan, specifically the Artorian people and the worlds they had inhabited and those they still held control over. He didn't waste time with disparaging remarks about their Jalvian neighbors, instead focusing on the achievements and struggles of his people.

"You have a very solid grasp of history for a soldier," I said after calling our lesson to a halt. My eyes were getting tired, and he'd given me a lot of information to process.

After verifying that our course was on track and any notifications would be forwarded to my room, I nodded toward the doorway. He took a couple of steps in that direction, but halted as soon as he realized I wasn't following. Apparently, he wasn't yet ready to give up his attempt to win my favor.

I wasn't against him trying, but there was a hint of desperation on him now and my gut said to lock the controls just in case. I quick set the command to shut out the controls to anyone but me and then caught up with Chesser.

He fell into step with me, but slowed our pace to a halting walk. "I didn't always want to be a soldier. That was a necessity." His gaze dipped to his hands. "I wanted to be an instructor at our local academy. My father had been one before the war had ramped up to a level that he'd had to join active duty when I was a kid, before my brother had even been born. Because of his background, my father spent a lot of his active-duty time consulting, working from a desk, so he could still come home at night. We were still a regular family then, when Vayen was little."

I had little experience with regular families. There were a few traditional human family units on the Verian station, but most children I knew of were raised by one parent or the other. Our transient nature often put us in dangerous places, leading to accidents, attacks, illness with poor medical care, or two people simply parting ways to follow different opportunities. Verians often exchanged their children for training at a young age, assuring each community had adequate generational coverage for necessary roles.

The way Chesser spoke of his family sounded like he sorely missed them. That part I understood.

His shoulders sagged. "More and more attacks were getting through to the ground, disrupting everyday life. No one could ignore it any longer. We couldn't pretend that war was a nebulous thing that happened far above the atmosphere, out of sight, a thing we only heard about on the news feeds at night."

"I know what you mean. I could see it from up on the station when Jalvians would come to raid Veria Prime or Minor, but after my family was killed, when I was on the surface in training, it was different. A lot of the populace couldn't be convinced that things were as dire as those of us who had seen it ourselves were trying to tell them. They didn't want to hear it. And then suddenly we were occupied. Then they cried out that we hadn't done enough to save them." I didn't bother to hide my disgust. As much as I loved the Verian people and those I'd grown up with, their blind optimism drove me insane.

"That is frustrating," he said, his hand settling on the small of my back, lightly, not pushing, just there.

We reached my room. He looked down the hall toward the cargo hold where his crew waited. I opened my door and followed his gaze for a moment before steeling myself to break my personal security rule. I stepped aside, gesturing for him to enter.

He didn't rush in, instead appearing hesitant for a few seconds before accepting my invitation. I closed the door and sat on the edge of the bed to take my shoes off.

"How did you end up a soldier?" I asked.

"When the violence escalated, everyone in the academy's teaching shifted from general studies to military. Many chose to go right into active duty after rudimentary training. Some of us stayed for more specialized instruction. My parents were both sent out into the action, as were many adults with any sort of military background. That left me to take care of my brother while they were gone. After the ship they'd served on was destroyed, he was all the family I had left. We don't come from a prolific line. We don't have a lot of wealth, but we're not as bad off as some."

"And your brother, what does he do when you're off on missions like this?"

Chesser sat beside me. He held a hand out to me. "We could talk all night, likely for an entire week, and I still might not convince you that we're different than the Jalvians."

"It's not that I need you to be different." I sighed. Trying to put my criteria into words was difficult. "I've spent time with them too. I heard their stories, about their families, their homes. It's not a cut and dry their-bad-and-you're-good situation." I eyed his still proffered open hand, but rubbed my face instead. "If I held this information back, your people would suffer greatly. If I give it to you, their people will suffer. My only win is getting them out of the Verian Cluster where they're causing havoc for the people I care about, but suffering still lands on my conscience."

His hand began to shake and his forehead creased as his gaze dropped from me to his lap. "Can I show you what you'd be saving if you help us?"

"When we get to Artor?"

He shook his head, sitting a little straighter. "My people, we can share memories. Your telepathy should allow it to work." He cleared his throat. "It's not something we do with others, only those very close to us. Memories are deeply personal."

If he thought he could sneak in while I was distracted with a pretty memory and steal the information from the meeting with General Zhan... "Would allowing this sharing give you access to my thoughts as well?"

"Only what you allow me access to. Or nothing. You could just view mine."

I buckled my defenses down just in case he was lying and slipped one hand into his. His rough thumb ran over my knuckles, back and forth, and his eyes closed. A nudge rubbed against my mind. Taking a chance that this wasn't a stealth invitation to a ransacking probe, I hesitantly followed his thoughts until our minds seemed to sync. In a disorienting shift of perspective, I became Chesser.

I walked into a kitchen of similar size to my suite on the Verian station, but warm sunlight filtered through two windows, adding a cheery glow to the warm tones of the room. A dark-haired young man sat at a wooden table, hunched over something with his back to me. Something seemed odd that I couldn't pin down for a few breaths, but then I realized it was the silence. The harder I listened, I picked up the faint sound of traffic, but inside the house, no air filters, no music, not even the hum of a cleaning bot.

I crept closer to the table. Pride and affection filling my mind along with the excitement being able to spend a few days home before my next assignment came in.

"Really, Vayen? Haven't they taught you to always be aware of your surroundings?" Chesser asked in an almost apologetic tone as he thought to himself how badly he was going to scare his brother by sneaking in.

The young man leapt up from his seat, cracking one knee painfully against the table leg as he spun to get up. Though he stood a few inches shorter, his face was nearly identical to the man sharing this memory with me. Younger, softer, yet a solemness in his dark eyes and bearing belied his age. "You're home!" he shouted, wincing as he rushed forward to wrap his arms around me.

I hugged him for a long moment until he had what he needed from me. He spent weeks at a time alone, sometimes longer. Instructors at the academy were no replacement for family, and though he assured me he had friends, he didn't mention spending time with them outside of classes.

"Tell me everything. Well, not everything, but what you can," he said eagerly.

Vayen prodded me toward a door down a hallway that led to our yard. He always knew I craved the green place after a mission. The door creaked as it slid open. I glimpsed an enclosed overgrown yard before bright sunlight blinded me for a second.

When my vision cleared, I stood shorter than before, and ran in circles, chasing a boy barely half my size as he giggled, running over thick green grass. The smell of it having been just trimmed filled the air. A woman with the same brown skin and dark hair, tended a garden, her hands and knees covered in dirt. She shook her head and laughed at us.

"You could just buy all that, you know," said a male voice behind me. "Save yourself the trouble."

"It tastes better when you grow it yourself," she playfully lobbed something round and orange in the direction of the voice.

Chesser's memory fell away as one of my own abruptly took over, as if on autopilot. Tumbling uncertainly from his memory into mine, I grabbed ahold of his mind, dragging him with me in the hopes of an anchoring force.

"It tastes better when you grow it yourself, Ana. That's why we do this." My father crouched in front of me, his face stern, his big hands engulfing my shoulders. "If you want your friends on the station to be healthy, you'll quit crying about being away from them, and be of some use here. Take these samples to your brother. Watch what he does closely, and maybe, one day, when you're older, you can work with us to make sure everyone can grow their own food."

My father brushed his knees off as he stood and then picked up a plas box, its partitions full of root cuttings. He handed it to me. My thin six-year-old arms held it steady, determined not to let him see how they wanted to shake under the weight of the box that was nearly as long as the spread of my arms.

"When people have their own food, they don't need to rely on others for survival. That allows them to be free. People who don't have to fight for resources are more likely to be at peace. Our work is important." He patted my head and gave me a little push. "Go on."

I opened my eyes, escaping the memory sharing with a pounding heart and feeling lightheaded. I wanted nothing more than to shove Chesser out my door so I could get myself under control, but my hands were shaking and he could already feel that through the one he was now squeezing. There was nowhere to hide.

"Anastassia?"

"I'm—"

"Do *not* say you're fine." He squeezed a little harder. "It's all right not to be all the time, you know."

I nodded, unwilling to admit he might be right with actual words. He'd given me enough of those for one day.

After all the years of my father being gone and never feeling close to him but missing him all the same, my memory had done a deep dive for what I needed to hear. I couldn't even imagine what he'd think of me now or knowing that his words eighteen years ago would be hopefully paving the way to the peace he'd been trying to provide to people who weren't even ours then or now.

Chesser wrapped one arm around me. He spoke quietly, as though he didn't want to interrupt whatever might be going on in my head. "Vayen is sixteen and studying at the same academy I did. He keeps wanting to enlist. I keep convincing him to stay home and study, but I don't know how much longer I can do that. We're desperate for every able body to join." He sighed deeply. "This war needs to end before I lose anyone else to it."

He sighed and cleared his throat. "I suppose you'll tell me the Jalvian soldiers feel the same way."

They did.

This war wasn't just about food or other resources and I held no delusions of a quick victory or an easy solution even with the information I held, but if I could eventually get in the room with the top assholes on both sides, I might be able to mediate a middle ground. If I could get anyone to listen to me. That was going to take a lot of balls throwing caution out the window, but hell, I'd never gained anything without taking a chance.

"I'll help you end it."

He leaned down to kiss me. I met him halfway.

My bed was exactly big enough for me and an Artorian man, if he didn't mind half his ass hanging over the edge. From the contented smile on his face, I didn't think he minded.

We'd spent seven hours in my room without interruption. Chesser had eagerly acted on the images I'd shown him as we tangled mind to mind and I was feeling quite content as well. Even my sore muscles were relaxed.

"I should go check see where we are, if we're close enough to send a secure message," he said.

I nodded, watching this man who was growing on me with each minute we spent together slide out of bed and fasten his shirt. Though he'd kept his pants on, and he'd seemed shy about me getting anywhere near him in that regard, he'd been thoroughly engaged and attentive in every other way. I was pretty sure that, given some time, I'd get him past his social conditioning. For now, I was quite happy to experiment with what we'd been sharing between us.

He gave me one last kiss and then left my bedroom. That was just as well. I needed some time to figure out what I was going to do once that secure channel was established.

Twenty minutes of unresolved thoughts, a change of clothes, and a trip to the bathroom to freshen up later, I met Chesser at the control panel. He handed me one of the meal bars I always kept on hand.

"Mox was still sleeping. He's the only one of us good in the kitchen. Thank Geva you have a sizeable stock of these. They're not too bad."

"Are we close enough?" I asked, unlocking the controls and peeling the wrapper back to take a bite.

"We will be in an hour."

Chesser used that time to delve back into the ship's database. He pulled up each inhabited world in the Narvan. He explained that Artor and Jal were the only ones that were naturally inhabitable and how his people had used their tech and their engineering skills to transform the others. Some worlds, like Rok, that had been taken from the Artorians early in the conflict, were only habitable due to immense domes that protected the people from hostile atmospheres. We were discussing the satellite web around Artor and how it controlled everything from the weather to air temperatures, when the notification Chesser had set pinged.

We were in range.

The more warning his people had, the better off they would be. It was one thing to tell them of the plan so they weren't caught by surprise, but if I helped them now, if I gave them everything, they could mount an offensive and be the ones to take the Jalvian force by surprise. If they had enough of a force left to hit them hard and fast, I would be that much closer to the possibility of sitting at the negotiation table with General Zhan and whoever Artor offered. He'd worked with me once before. I hoped he would again.

I stared at the planets on the display still glowing before me. The same worlds I'd seen in General Nalaton's simulation. There were no blue or orange shimmers, just planets filled with people. People I could save.

"I want someone who can make assurances. Can you get me that?"

I suddenly had Chesser's full attention. "Is what you have as valuable as you make it out to be? If I set this meeting up and this is old information or insignificant, I'm going to lose my credibility. My career will be over."

"Your career will be just fine. And yes, if you want to hit the Jalvians hard enough that they will be willing to eventually negotiate rather than obliterate you, I've got what you need."

Excitement lit in his face. I felt it bubbling inside me too. If I could use my training to help broker peace between entire worlds, maybe that would be better than the future serving the Verian people in robes that I'd failed at. Maybe Res was wrong. It wasn't that I wasn't good enough. Veria Prime just wasn't where I was meant to be.

I finished my meal bar while he set up the connection. When that was established, Chesser flew into a rapid-fire conversation in his language with the floating head and shoulders that hovered over the panel between us. That face was replaced by another and then another until the fourth one, an Artorian male with greying hair and deep creases around his eyes, addressed Chesser.

When the conversation switched to Trade, I stepped up beside him. "If I give you this, if you successfully thwart their attack and drive them into submission, I want an agreement that you will send aid to the Verian Cluster. You will remove all Jalvian presence there and then leave. We are happy to trade, but all Narvan occupation of the Verian worlds and their subsidiary holdings will cease."

His face grew grim. "Our resources are low. Even if we, by the grace of Geva, may be victorious in the coming battle, our forces will be depleted even further."

Having dealt with General Zhan during the treaty negotiations, I'd learned that negotiations outside of the Verian people required far more force. Perhaps even threats before a level of cooperation could be reached.

"My forces *are* depleted. Driven into the ground, in fact. Whatever you have at the end of this will help restore order. You owe us that for bringing your Narvan drama into our damned space. We wanted no part in this."

He scowled. The projection wavered. I thought we'd maybe lost him, but then it recovered. "We are not the ones occupying your homeworld."

"You're all one people in my book, so you can either clean up after yourselves or suffer what the Jalvians have in store for you."

Chesser glared at me. I waved him away. He'd done his part and gotten me this meeting. The rest was up to me.

"We don't take kindly to threats." The man slipped into Artorian, likely venting to Chesser.

I cut him off. "I don't take kindly to having my family killed in your fucking conflict or having my life turned upside down because your war spilled over into the Verian Cluster. Commit to fixing it and I will give you what you need right now."

"All of it?" Chesser asked, hope dripping off every syllable.

"Yes, all of it."

Chesser spoke Artorian again, nodding at me several times. The man listened, interjecting only twice.

The projection went still. I turned to Chesser.

"He's conferring with his advisors."

"Who is this guy? Can he actually do what I'm asking, or will some-one overrule him tomorrow?"

Chesser shook his head and chuckled. "Anastassia, you're grinding the balls of the Premiere of all of Artor. I don't think anyone is going to dare overrule him."

"Oh." Heat rushed over my face. "You could have said something."

"And tamed what you needed to say to get your deal? Oh, hells no." He grinned. "I couldn't get away with any of that, but I enjoy watching you work."

The head reanimated. "You have your deal."

"Thank you, sir." I said, in a far too late attempt to make up for my entire lapse in protocol. "To whom should I relay the information?"

The head vanished, to be replaced by the view of a host of Artorian men and women seated around one end of a table. There were too many faces for the projection to simulate. They all acted as one oddly distorted image.

A female voice spoke in Artorian. I looked to Chesser.

"They're asking me to translate. I doubt fork is going to come up much in this conversation."

I grinned and then closed my eyes to recount the conversation that had happened in meeting room six of the Verian station in as much detail as my Seeker training had prepared me to recall.

When we'd finished, two hours had passed. My mouth had gone dry after so much talking. Chesser wrapped up in Artorian and then the projection evaporated, leaving us alone in the control room.

His dark gaze locked onto me in that way that made my stomach flip. "You've saved my people, Anastassia. They won't forget this."

"They better not."

Chesser reached out and took my hand. "You should stay so they don't. Not that they will. I mean, your name will be in our history for-ever for helping us end this." He took a quick breath and licked his lips. "What I mean to ask is if you will consider staying on Artor with me. As part of my team. Or not. Your choice. I like this, what we have started. If you're willing, I'd like to see where we might go."

"Together, or as part of your team?"

"Yes?" The wicked grin he flashed me was full of ideas of where we might go.

I threw my head back and laughed.

There were far worse places to be than on a beautiful world with perfect weather, grateful people, and a man who made me smile. If it didn't pan out, I could return to the station once the Premiere kept his word. I deserved a chance to be happy, didn't I?

"What's the Artorian word for happy?"

"*Dshva.*"

I tried to pronounce it, but it sounded so wrong that I gave up on the third attempt. "Staying with you on Artor would make me whatever you said."

He laughed. "We'll work on your Artorian. Everything else will fall into place."

If we could put this war to rest, I couldn't see how it wouldn't. Surely grand adventures waited for me on this new world with Chesser by my side.

THE NARVAN CONTINUES WITH:

TRUST

BOOK 1

Loud voices inside the house brought me to a pause on the front step. One belonged to my brother. The other to a woman, likely the one he'd been seeing that I'd never met. My hand hovered over the door controls. Staying outside and out of their argument would be wise.

The last time we two brothers had gotten into it, the neighbors had called the enforcers. I hoped they didn't feel so inclined this time around. I didn't need any additional questionable behavior tainting my otherwise commendable record.

I glanced up at the sky. A few fluffy white clouds dotted the vast blueness, giving no indication of the war raging on outside the atmosphere. There hadn't been any ground attacks in a couple weeks. I prayed to Geva that Artor was finally making some progress against Jal. The war had already taken my parents and so many others. We needed to end this, soon, before I lost my brother, too.

Out of school early thanks to a canceled class, Chesser wouldn't have expected me to be home yet. Did he bring Anastassia here often while I was gone? He was only on leave for another two days. Her too, for that matter, since he'd recruited her to his team.

It would be a month or more before I saw him again. His off time was supposed to be our time together, to pretend we were still a family for a few days, a little dose of what I vaguely remembered as normal. But since he'd met Anastassia, they were inseparable. Elsewhere. They were together the whole time he was on duty. Wasn't that enough?

I wasn't opposed to him seeing anyone and I'd made that quite clear, but he still made no effort to get the two of us in the same room. Maybe she was ugly, but it sure didn't sound like his friends gave him any grief about her.

The argument inside elevated to all out shouting. I leaned in closer to the door.

"Why wouldn't you want children?" Chesser asked.

"Why would I? I'm not about to give up my life to sit around here and personally replenish your homeworld's population. Besides, who knows if we're even compatible that way."

"We are. I received a confirmation from the inquiry I had submitted to the University."

"You made a fucking inquiry?" Her voice rose, breaking from the steady malice she'd been slinging at my brother.

Something hit the wall next to the door and thudded to the floor. Great, one of them was throwing things. At least it didn't sound like anything breakable.

"Bearing children is an honor. This isn't some little rustic utopia like Veria Prime where everyone reproduces on a whim. I'm cleared to continue my family line, and I'd rather not see it end with me and Vayen."

My teeth ground together. He hadn't even seen fit to introduce me to this woman, but he intended to join with her and they were talking children already?

Oh Geva, that meant he'd bonded with her! That wasn't something that could be undone.

She wasn't even Artorian for Geva's sake. Similar, and naturally telepathic like us, but not the same. My mother would have had a fit about him even considering bringing half-breed children into our line.

If any of what he told me about the missions he did were true, he probably had gained a few favors from fairly high up the chain of command, but I rather doubted even that was enough to get the government to overlook Anastassia's genetics.

"Then Vayen can continue your family line. Leave me out of it," she said with all the finality of an official decree.

"He's only sixteen." There was a single loud thump that I hoped was Chesser slamming his hand on the countertop or table and not a fist through a wall that I'd have to fix. "It will be another six years before he's eligible for the procedure. With the war going on, who knows if he'll make it that long. At this rate, I won't. Anastassia, I need to know this is taken care of."

Chesser couldn't die. He was all the family I had left.

As I stood outside, heart pounding, ear pressed to the door, I became increasingly aware of inquiring gazes from those passing by on the street. One of the round news feed bots whizzed by, hopefully chasing down some celebrity or government official and not an indication that another attack was about to happen. Traffic overhead was minimal at this hour, but if I stood here much longer, someone was going to file a suspicious activity report.

Despite the continued shouting, I keyed in my entry code and stepped into the kitchen. Modestly sized, the room was not near large enough to contain the tension that skyrocketed upon the two of them spotting me.

Chesser halted mid-curse to force a smile in my direction. "You're home early."

My mind raced, debating whether to join in the fray or escape to my room. The red-faced woman with narrowed green eyes who was gripping the countertop as though she wanted to tear it from the wall decided it for me. If this went any further beyond shouting, someone would be calling in the enforcers and it might even be me.

I slid the bag off my shoulder and dropped it onto the table in the middle of the room. "You're supposed to be ending this war, not dying in it," I said. "How can you even consider having a kid right now? Half the cities on Artor are running at half power thanks to the last round of ground attacks. Ours is one of them, which is why I'm home by the way. Not that you've probably even noticed the power rationing in that dingy hole of a bar that you'd rather hang out in than be here."

The subtle smile that spread across Anastassia's lips interrupted the venting spree I was just getting started on. She wasn't ugly, but not exactly stunning either.

Not being familiar with her kind, I could only guess her age, based on her appearance, was somewhere between Chesser and I. Now that she appeared calmer, it became clear her skin was naturally pale, a stark contrast to our coloring. Chesser had mentioned finding her on Veria Prime but she didn't appear to be related to them either. She came from one of the transient races. I half-remembered Chesser saying that her kind always looked for home elsewhere or something bigger and better. Which made me seriously wonder why she was here, with him, in the middle of a war.

Available in print and ebook from your favorite online retailer
Signed copies are available at JeanDavisAuthor.com (within the US)

About the Author

Jean Davis writes an array of speculative fiction and plays with chickens. When not ruining fictional lives from the comfort of her writing chair, she can be found devouring books and sushi, weeding her flower garden, or picking up hundreds of sticks while attempting to avoid the abundant snake population that also shares her yard. She lives in West Michigan with her musical husband, an attention-craving terrier, and a small flock of chickens and ducks

Find links to all of her books, updates on new projects, and sign up for her mailing list at www.jeandavisauthor.com. You'll also find her on Facebook and Instagram at JeanDavisAuthor, and on Goodreads and Amazon.

If you enjoyed this book, please consider leaving a review. They are much appreciated. Thank you!

Made in the USA
Monee, IL
23 July 2024